The Case of the Time-Capsule Bandit

RANDI RHODES
NINJA DETECTIVE

The Case of the Time-Capsule Bandit

By OCTAVIA SPENCER

Simon & Schuster Books for Young Readers

New York   London   Toronto   Sydney   New Delhi

SIMON & SCHUSTER BOOKS FOR YOUNG READERS
An imprint of Simon & Schuster Children's Publishing Division
1230 Avenue of the Americas, New York, New York 10020

SIMON & SCHUSTER BOOKS FOR YOUNG READERS is a trademark of Simon & Schuster, Inc.
For information about special discounts for bulk purchases, please contact Simon & Schuster
Special Sales at 1-866-506-1949 or business@simonandschuster.com.
The Simon & Schuster Speakers Bureau can bring authors to your live event. For more
information or to book an event, contact the Simon & Schuster Speakers Bureau
at 1-866-248-3049 or visit our website at www.simonspeakers.com.
Book design and diagram drawings by Chloë Foglia
The text for this book is set in Janson Text LT Std.
The illustrations for this book are rendered digitally.
Manufactured in the United States of America
0913 FFG
2 4 6 8 10 9 7 5 3 1
Library of Congress Cataloging-in-Publication Data
Spencer, Octavia.
The case of the time-capsule bandit / Octavia Spencer ; [illustrations, Vivienne To].
p. cm. — (Randi Rhodes, ninja detective ; [1])
Summary: Twelve-year-old Randi, unhappy about moving from Brooklyn to Deer Creek,
Tennessee, after her mother's death, soon finds new friends and a case to solve surrounding a
stolen time capsule and rumors of a centuries-old treasure.
ISBN 978-1-4424-7681-3 (hardcover)
[1. Mystery and detective stories. 2. Community life—Tennessee—Fiction. 3. Single-parent
families—Fiction. 4. Moving, Household—Fiction. 5. Time capsules—Fiction. 6. Buried
treasure—Fiction. 7. Tennessee—Fiction.] I. To, Vivienne, ill. II. Title.
PZ7.S74817Cas 2013
[Fic]—dc23
2012037405
ISBN 978-1-4424-7683-7 (eBook)

To my mom, for fostering my desire to learn
and for being the angel on my shoulder

ACKNOWLEDGMENTS

Thanks to my family, all of my nieces and nephews, Kelly Shipe, Peggy and Jerry Shipe, Andy McNicol, Brad Slater, Brian Clisham, Melissa Kates, Bria Schreiber, Rick Sutton, and Zareen Jaffery.

CHAPTER ONE

THE FINAL CASE

Gotcha! Randi Rhodes thought. *Now smile real big for the camera.*

Down on the sidewalk, three stories below her bedroom window, the man in the navy suit checked over his shoulder to make sure no one was watching. It was six o'clock on a Friday morning. Most of Randi's Brooklyn neighbors were still snuggled up in their beds, but Randi had gotten up at the crack of dawn, just as she had for the past three days. She'd been on a stakeout for over an hour, never budging from her post while she waited for the man to show up with his dog.

Randi snapped several photos of the man and a few more of his prissy white Pekingese. And when the pair hurried off around the corner, she zoomed in for a close-up of the mess that the dastardly villains had left behind. The pretty pink tulips she'd planted as bait in front of her house had been ripped up at the roots. The only things left behind were a hole in the ground and a sprinkling of soil on the sidewalk.

How many gardens have you destroyed? she thought. *How many old ladies have woken up to find their pansies plucked and their rose-bushes ransacked? How many kids won't get to enjoy the first flowers they ever helped plant? How many lives have you made a little less beautiful? All because you're too cheap to buy your flowers from a florist.*

Randi downloaded the photos onto her computer and printed out a few of the best. The man in the pictures lived three blocks away. He'd been her prime suspect for quite some time. Front-yard flowers had been disappearing every morning since the man and his family had moved into the neighborhood. However, until now, the evidence against him had been *circumstantial*. Finally, Randi had *proof*.

Another case closed. Randi congratulated herself. She folded the pictures and stuffed them into an envelope. Then she typed out a note on her computer.

Dear Sir,

At 6:10 a.m. on the morning of June 15th, you were photographed stealing tulips from a garden on Bergen Street. Since you're new to the neighborhood, you might not be aware that there are many fine florists within a few blocks of your home. From now on, please visit one of these businesses whenever you want a few freshly cut flowers. If you keep "weeding" your neighbors' front yards, I'll make sure that every gardener in Brooklyn knows who to thank.

Randi rooted through her desk for her favorite pen, a blue ballpoint with a chewed-up cap she'd found among her mom's old things. She signed the letter *Glenn Street*.

A few hours later, with her belly full of breakfast, Randi shoved the envelope into the back pocket of her jeans and set off to make the delivery.

"Hey!" her dad called when he heard the front door open. "Where ya going?"

"Just for a walk around the block," Randi told him. "I'll be right back."

"I hope so," he said. "We're leaving on Sunday and you haven't even packed."

Randi frowned. "I'm waiting for you to change your mind."

"Not going to happen. So don't disappear. And, hon?"

"What?"

"*Please*. Be careful!"

Be careful? Randi thought miserably as she stomped down the street. *I'm not the one you should be worried about. What's going to happen to the neighborhood if you drag me away? I keep these streets clean. I take the cases that the NYPD won't bother with. Who else is going to catch all the litterbugs? Who's going to bring Brooklyn's bullies, plant snatchers, and pigeon nappers to justice?*

When she reached the man's house, she could see his white Pekingese peeping out of the parlor window. A vase filled with pretty pink tulips sat on a table next to the sofa. Randi scrambled up the building's stoop and shoved her envelope through the mail slot. In the past, she would have tried to be more discreet. *Who cares if they ID me? I'm leaving Brooklyn forever. Besides, maybe it's time everyone knows I'm the real Glenn Street.*

It stung a bit to think that none of the neighbors had ever figured it out. Randi might have solved thirty-two cases, but adults just saw a tall kid with knobby knees; fiery red ringlets; and a freckled, moon-shaped face. They never saw the real Miranda Rhodes. Most people in the neighborhood believed Randi's dad was Brooklyn's mysterious watchdog. After all, Glenn Street was the heroine of his bestselling detective books. But Herb Rhodes would usually laugh out loud whenever the subject was raised. He claimed he was flattered that a crime-fighting vigilante had decided to borrow his character's name.

Randi wondered how he'd feel if he ever found out that the vigilante in question was his twelve-year-old daughter. ☠

☠ Go to Appendix A to complete the first Ninja Task!

CHAPTER TWO

GOOD-BYE, LIFE

"Miranda, time to go!" Randi heard her father shouting from downstairs. She was still in her room, packing the last of her belongings.

This is it. Randi shut her suitcase and grabbed her hat off the bed. She paused in front of the closet-door mirror and shoved her vintage fedora down over her curls. *Your life is finished,* she informed her reflection.

"Miranda!"

"Coming!"

Randi tucked her favorite Glenn Street novel into her backpack and did one last check of the closet. Stacked against the back wall was her collection of *Detective Weekly* magazines. She sighed at the sight. Her days as a detective were over; that much was clear. She'd planned to leave the magazines for the new owner's two kids. *Maybe one of them can be the next Glenn Street,* she had thought. *Or maybe they would join forces. There was definitely enough work in the neighborhood for two vigilantes.*

But there was always a chance Randi's magazine collection would end up tossed in the trash. And that, she realized, was a risk she just couldn't take.

She crammed the dusty magazines into her suitcase, and an eighteen-month-old copy slid out and fell to the floor. On the front was a photo of Randi's dad. He'd made the cover of *Detective Weekly* six times. The edition that had just landed next to Randi's feet was the only one she'd refused to read. RHODES RETIRES! screamed the headline. *Will this be the end of Glenn Street?* Randi solemnly studied the picture. People used to say that she looked like her mom, because they shared the same curly red hair. No one ever seemed to notice that Randi had inherited everything else from her dad.

Outside, a car horn blared three times in a row. It was her dad's code for *Get a move on!* Randi rolled up the magazine and took one last look around her empty room. Her fingers felt for the tiny silver heart that hung around her neck. "Good-bye, Mom," Randi whispered. Then she reluctantly lugged her suitcase downstairs.

As her father's car pulled away from the curb, Randi glanced back at the brownstone that had been their home for all twelve years of her life. She half expected to see her mom on the front stoop, her curls blowing in the wind while she waved good-bye. That's where she'd stood in the months before she died, after she'd gotten too weak to walk Randi to school. That was a year ago. Now there was nobody there.

"You okay, princess?" her father asked. He always seemed to squirm when he tried to talk about feelings.

Randi nodded and turned her face to the window, attempting to swallow the lump that had formed in the back of her throat.

Princess? she could almost hear Glenn Street say. *You think I'm some sweet little girl? Where have you been for the past year, buddy? Want to know how many cases I solved last week alone? Five. That's right.* Five. *I've been protecting south Brooklyn since early last summer. And what were you doing? I'll tell you what you were doing. Nothing. You were so busy doing nothing that you even stopped writing. And that's when I figured I had to start reading. Here's what I learned from your books: Not all girls turn out to be pretty little princesses. Some grow up to be tough—just like Glenn Street. Why can't you see that your own kid is one of them?*

Randi chewed on her lower lip. Her dad never would have treated a boy like some delicate flower. Calling her *princess* or *sweetheart* or *honey* or *hon.* Worrying every time she left the house for five minutes. It didn't even make sense! She'd been taking Tae Kwon Do since the second grade. Two years ago, she'd earned a black belt. Randi remembered how thrilled she'd been when Sensei Daniel had asked her to perform at the ceremony. She couldn't wait to show her dad just how good she'd gotten. But he'd had to leave on a book tour early that morning, and he couldn't be there to watch. Randi's mom found her crying after the exhibition was over. Somehow her mom's hug had made everything better.

Crying was the last thing Randi wanted to do right now, but she suddenly needed one of those hugs. Randi pulled the fedora down over her eyes and blinked back the tears. She had loved being a kid when her mom was around. They'd had so much fun. Now there would be no more bike rides through Central Park to collect fall leaves for the Thanksgiving center-piece. No games of I Spy as they walked along Fifth Avenue at Christmastime, watching window dressers transform store-fronts into winter-wonder delights. Randi would especially miss the gingerbread brownstones they used to build on Christmas Eve. But that was kid stuff. She'd had to toughen up in the past year. Life was different now that it was just her and her dad.

Randi glanced over at her father. He was long and lanky— just like her. His hair and skin were darker, but they shared the same eyes. Yet it often felt like she hardly knew him—and that he didn't know her at all. He'd traveled so much when she was little. His "ready" suitcase had always been packed and hidden in the closet for the next book tour or research trip. That had stopped the day they found out Randi's mother was ill. Herb Rhodes had quit writing the moment he'd heard. He informed his publisher that Glenn Street was over, and for six straight months, he'd barely left the house. He'd told Randi it was his job to take care of the girl that he'd married. He tried to do it all by himself, even though he could have hired a nurse to help. He must have felt bad for spending so much time away from home. As far as Randi was concerned, he *should* have felt bad.

Her father gave Randi a pat on the head. "It's going to be all right, kiddo. We've talked about this. You'll love living in Deer Creek year-round."

I'll hate it, she told herself. Randi and her parents had spent every summer in Deer Creek, Tennessee. The tiny town was a nice place to visit. But eight weeks of vacation were more than enough. Now Randi was going to be stuck in the mountains *forever.* It just wasn't right. She didn't belong in the boondocks. She was a born-and-bred city girl. A native New Yorker, as her mom used to say.

She'd understand, Randi thought as a tear trickled down her cheek. She quickly wiped it away. Her mom had always told her it was good to cry. She was the sort of person who'd get weepy if Randi finished a hard jigsaw puzzle or brought home a decent report card. But Randi couldn't remember a single moment when she'd seen her dad cry. He hadn't even cried the night her mother had died.

Tough guys don't cry, Randi reminded herself. *Get it together. You're not a kid anymore. You're a black belt. A detective. You're Glenn Street. And remember the most important thing about her?*

"Glenn Street never cries." Randi heard her lips say it out loud.

Her father shot her a worried look. "Hon, you know Glenn Street doesn't cry because she's not a real person," he said.

"She's real to me," Randi replied.

"She's just a silly character, sweetie. Glenn Street barely has two dimensions . . ." Herb's voice trailed off.

"Doesn't matter," Randi replied. "She's still the coolest woman I've ever known."

"You're wrong about that. Your mother was a million times . . . uh . . . cooler." Her father choked back an unexpected sob on the last word. To Randi, it just sounded like he was clearing his throat. He'd been doing that a lot lately. "Listen, there's something I need to talk to you about," he said, changing the subject.

"What?" Randi asked, narrowing her eyes just like Glenn did when she questioned a bad guy.

"Remember Mei-Ling Cooper? Her husband was a carpenter at the Museum of Natural History? The lady who helped me with the research I did for the Hong Kong scenes in *The China Connection*? She babysat you a few times."

"Yeah, I remember. What about her?" Randi said snippily. She remembered the old lady—and she knew exactly where this was going.

"Her husband passed away a while back, and she's been looking for regular work. So she's going to spend some time with us in Deer Creek, maybe stay and look after you . . . I mean *us*. I've heard she's quite the cook."

"Then she should get a job at a restaurant. I don't need any-one looking after me," Randi said flatly. *End of subject.*

Her father gave Randi an uneasy glance and then turned

his eyes back to the road. They traveled in silence while Randi thumbed through the pages of the latest *Detective Weekly*. She was only pretending to read so she'd have an excuse not to talk. Then an ad in the classifieds section grabbed her attention.

She had to have it. Her old detective kit was running low on supplies. There wouldn't be many cases to solve in sleepy Deer Creek, but that BPX5 bike sure might come in handy. And for once she could actually afford it. Somewhere in the trunk of the car was a piggy bank crammed with Randi's entire life savings—$207.18. Randi tore out the page and tucked it into her pocket just as her dad turned the car into the Holland Tunnel.

In front of them was a Prius with suitcases and sleeping bags bungeed to its roof. Three kids and a sheltie were crammed into the backseat. Randi wondered if they were being exiled to Tennessee, too.

"Looks like they're heading off on a camping trip," her dad

said, breaking the silence. "Probably get in a lot of fishing with all those boys."

"They're going camping, all right, but they won't be doing any fishing with those *girls*," Randi corrected him.

"Interesting theory, Madame Detective. How do you know that they're girls?" Randi's dad challenged her. "All you can see is the tops of their heads."

"There's a sticker on the back bumper that says *Hewitt*. That's a girls-only school in Manhattan. There are three flowery suitcases on top of the car. And no boy alive would ever let the family dog wear a collar like *that*."

Her father grinned when he noticed the dog's twinkling rhinestone collar. "So they're girls. What makes you so sure they're not going fishing?"

"No fishing rods. The Prius's trunk is too small to hold them, and they're not up top with the suitcases."

Her father's grin widened. "Masterful deduction," he said, giving his best Sherlock Holmes impression.

"Simple observation," Randi replied, cracking a smile for the first time that day.

The smile faded the second they emerged from the tunnel. Randi peered over her shoulder as the city—her city—grew smaller in the distance. A thumb-size Lady Liberty waved a lonesome good-bye. Randi hoped she'd be able to remember that magnificent skyline, with its skyscrapers shimmering in the white sunlight.

So long, New York. She turned back around to face the long stretch of highway in front of her. "So long, life," Randi muttered.

"What was that?" her father asked.

"Nothing." She shoved her hand into her pocket. At least she had the BPX5 ad. And that meant Randi Rhodes still had one little thing to look forward to.

CHAPTER THREE

SPOOKY

The gravel crunched under the wheels of the rusty old Schwinn Randi had been riding since she'd gotten to Deer Creek a week earlier. She tried to change gears and grumbled when the shifter refused to budge. She couldn't wait for her brand-new BPX5 to come in the mail. Her dad's bike was just as ancient as Randi's—not that he seemed to mind. He pedaled down the mountain lane with a grin on his face. For the first time in a year, Herb Rhodes looked genuinely happy.

Even Randi had to admit that summer in the Smokies could be magical. Deer Creek was nestled in a remote valley between two mountains. The road from the family house into town ran along the Tuckaseegee, a catfish-rich river that had once been a popular tourist draw. On their side of the river, the Guyton Orchard was already producing the juicy red apples Randi had once loved. On the opposite side of the Tuckaseegee sat a row of charming vacation cottages. Families from across the country used to journey to Deer

Creek for the stunning mountain scenery, the mild climate, and the legendary fishing. In recent years, though, the village had been all but forgotten. Now the cabins on the far side of the river all posted VACANCY signs.

"I remember the days when there'd be fifty kids splashing around over there," she heard her father say wistfully. "Your mom and I must have jumped off that old dock a thousand times."

Randi's mother and father had met in Deer Creek when they were both teenagers. Ten years later, they'd married at the church in town, and they'd bought a house here right after Randi was born. Every summer the family had returned to the mountains. Then last June, Randi's mom had died, and the two remaining Rhodeses had spent the summer season in Brooklyn. In the two years since Randi had last biked past her parents' old vacation spot, the place seemed to have slid a bit closer toward ruin. The cottages desperately needed a fresh coat of paint, and the crumbling dock looked ready to wash away.

"Wouldn't recommend setting foot on that dock now," Randi mumbled. "It would probably fall in on top of you."

"It's not looking so sturdy, is it?" her father agreed. "Maybe they'll fix it up next. Just wait till you see what they've done to the town!"

Randi shot her dad a halfhearted smile. Seven whole days had passed since they had arrived in Deer Creek. Their moving vans had come and gone. The unpacking had kept Randi busy at first, but once the boxes were empty, she'd fallen into a funk. She stayed in her room, thumbing through *Detective Weekly* and rereading old case files. Her father had been trying for days to get her out of the house, as if some fresh air might cure her condition. But Randi was pretty sure that the boredom was terminal. A ride into the dullest town on earth wasn't going to do much to save her.

"Now start pedaling faster," her dad called out as he picked up speed. "We have to get there in time to see them take out the time capsule!"

Digging up an old box. That's what passes for excitement in a town like Deer Creek.

"Yeah, we wouldn't want to miss *that*, would we?"

Randi's father ignored the sarcasm. "This year, the Founders' Day Festival is a really big deal. Deer Creek is turning two hundred years old, and I have it on good authority that a *very* important person is going to be here in town for the celebration next Sunday."

"What kind of big shot's going to come out here to the middle of nowhere?" Randi sniffed.

"Well, it must be *someone* special, because they're giving him the honor of opening the capsule. I've heard all sorts of legends about the town's three founders. Who knows what they might have buried two hundred years ago. The VIP could crack open that box and find a real treasure inside."

"Him?"

"Excuse me?"

"You said him. VIPs can be female, too, you know," Randi pointed out.

"Yes, I *do* know. It's just that I have a hunch who our VIP's going to be. And if I'm right, this one is a *guy*."

"Who do you think it is?"

"Someone who vacationed here once back when he was a boy. Remember that story your mom used to tell?"

Randi had heard it a thousand times. Her mother always bragged that she'd taught the future President of the United States how to fish the summer they both turned twelve.

"You're trying to tell me that *President Gordon* is coming down here for the Deer Creek Founders' Day Festival," Randi scoffed.

"I sure hope so. Imagine what it would mean for the town if the celebration ends up all over the news. It could bring a whole new generation of families back to these mountains."

You go ahead and hope, Dad, Randi thought. *I don't mess around with wishes or rumors. I only deal with cold, hard facts.*

"Listen up." A vehicle was driving up fast behind them. "Maybe that's the president now," Randi joked. She and her father pulled to the side of the narrow road to let the car pass by. But as the car approached, they saw that it was trailed by two others just like it. Three black SUVs with tinted windows raced past, their heavy wheels pelting Randi's bike with tiny pieces of gravel. None of the cars had license plates.

Spooks! She'd read about them in her dad's books. *What business could professional spies have in the mountains of east Tennessee?*

Randi hopped back on the bike and pumped hard on the pedals. A few minutes later, she and her father rolled into Deer Creek, where men in dark suits and sunglasses were already canvassing the town square. *Not spooks. Secret Service agents,* Randi thought. *Which means . . .*

She glanced up at her father in amazement. "The president really *is* coming to Deer Creek!"

CHAPTER FOUR

GONE

Deer Creek was bustling with activity. The heart of the village was Founders' Square, a circle-shaped park surrounded by a handful of shops, the local bank, two tiny cafés, and Prufrock's Ice Cream Parlor. Everyone in town seemed to be out in the square, preparing Deer Creek for its Founders' Day Festival.

They must have been working for months, Randi thought. Most of the town's buildings had been recently painted. Brightly colored flowers lined the sidewalks, and brand-new park benches were still waiting for someone to sit on them. The north side of the plaza even featured a farmers' market. There were apples from Guyton Orchard, freshly baked pies from Shipe's, the local bakery, and wildflower honey from the town sheriff's own hives. Deer Creek had always been cute, just a little rundown. Now it looked like a place right out of a fairy tale. Or it would have, if it were not for two things: McCarthy's Bait 'n' Tackle shop remained the unsightly hovel that Randi remembered. And there were burly men in dark suits stomping around the park, rounding up any ordinary citizens who'd gone ahead and claimed seats. A dozen townsfolk were brusquely ushered off the grass and onto the surrounding sidewalk. They chatted with one another while three of the Secret Service agents built a temporary fence around the unusual monument at the center of Founders' Square.

Back when she was little, Randi had loved to pretend that the monument was an enchanted castle. There was something bewitching about it. An enormous boulder hauled into town from one of the mountains, its surface was covered in tiny flecks that glittered in the sunlight. Anchored to the north side of the rock, a bronze plaque crafted by the town's three founders read, REMEMBER HOW IT ALL BEGAN.

"What are those Secret Service guys doing over there by the monument?" Randi asked her father as she watched the boulder disappear from view behind the agents' fence.

"They're protecting the boss, I'd imagine. The time capsule's buried under the boulder. If the president's going to open the capsule, they'll want to make sure it's not dangerous."

Randi pointed to a pair of men who were approaching the monument with crowbars and shovels. Another Secret Service agent drove a small backhoe over the grass. Even a bunch of muscular men would need a machine to uproot the massive rock. "The Secret Service is going to move the monument and dig up the capsule? Shouldn't people from Deer Creek get the honor? Their ancestors were the ones who buried the thing!"

"It does seem unfair, but I guess you can't be too safe," her father responded.

"Oh, come on," Randi huffed. "Does the Secret Service really think the three founders were plotting against President Gordon when they buried the capsule two hundred years ago?"

"No. It's entirely possible that the founders were plotting against each other, though. The Suttons, Prufrocks, and McCarthys have despised one another for ages. If there *is* some kind of treasure inside, I wouldn't be surprised if one of the founders booby-trapped the capsule in case the others decided to dig it up first. Mayor Landers is just trying to be cautious. He doesn't want anything going wrong on his watch."

"Yeah, we wouldn't want anything *interesting* to happen here in Dullsville," Randi droned. But the chance that she might get to see a two-hundred-year-old booby trap in action had already lightened her mood.

"The mayor's scheduled to unveil the capsule at noon. Then it goes straight to the jail for safekeeping. Looks like we have a few minutes before they get started. Can I tempt you away from all this excitement with some ice cream?"

"You can," Randi replied with a grin. But she didn't take her eyes off the Secret Service agents. While her dad stopped to chat with one of the locals, she walked her cycle to the bike rack near Prufrock's Ice Cream Parlor.

Betty Prufrock herself was standing on the sidewalk outside the shop. A hardy-looking woman with chubby pink cheeks, she was one of the two biggest gossips in town. The other, Sheriff Ogle, was leaning against a streetlight, devouring a triple-scoop cone. Randi had heard that the sheriff had once been a champion kickboxer. Now Deer Creek's only police officer was as round and pink as a jelly bean.

Randi could hear the pair chatting, and judging by the tone of their voices, Randi figured the gossip was extra juicy this morning. She crouched down behind the bike rack and pretended to futz with the lock.

"Selma told me Stevie Rogers almost got his arm ripped clean off," Mrs. Prufrock said. Randi snarled a little at the sound of the name. Stevie Rogers was nothing more than a half-grown thug. During her last trip to Deer Creek, he'd found out the hard way what happens when you try to "borrow" a bike from a black belt.

"You know how Selma exaggerates. But Stevie did come away with a nasty ol' bruise," the sheriff confirmed. "And I checked out the cabin right after it happened. Wasn't a soul inside."

"Well, the boy's got no one to blame but himself," Mrs. Prufrock said with a *tsk*. "He shouldn't have been fooling around in that old cabin at night. Everyone knows the whole Holler's haunted."

No exaggeration there, Randi thought. Even *she* knew Rock

Hollow was haunted. Just up the road from Deer Creek, at the base of one of the mountains, Rock Hollow was the site of one of the first cabins built in east Tennessee. The shack's last owner had been a crazy old codger by the name of Toot Anderson McCarthy. Toot had spent most of the 1980s on an endless treasure hunt. Then one day about twenty years back, he had vanished without a trace.

It was his spirit that was said to haunt the Rock Hollow cabin and the treacherous caves that riddled the mountain behind it. These days it was practically a Deer Creek tradition for teenagers to get chased off the property by Toot's ornery ghost.

"Still, never heard of old Toot hurting anybody before," Mrs. Prufrock added.

"Can't blame his ghost for being in a bad mood," the sheriff replied with a mouth full of ice cream. A thin stream of chocolate trickled down her chin. She wiped it away with the sleeve of her uniform. "Toot spent all those years looking for the Deer Creek treasure, and turns out, it was right here in town the whole time."

"You think there's treasure in the time capsule?" Mrs. Prufrock asked in a tone that seemed to imply that she *didn't*.

"Where else would it be?" said the sheriff.

"If you ask me, the Deer Creek treasure is nothing more than a legend. But if that silly old story is how the mayor convinced you-know-who to stop by for a visit, then I'm happy to play along. I just hope it's enough to save this godforsaken town," Mrs. Prufrock lamented.

"Betty, Sheriff, how are you ladies doing today?"

Randi recognized her father's voice and quickly stood up. She didn't want the two women to know she'd been spying.

"Look who's here. It's Herb and Miranda." Sheriff Ogle paused to take another lick off her chocolate cone. "You finally give up big-city life for some peace and quiet?"

"Who wants peace and quiet when you can have loud and dangerous?" Randi quipped.

"Never mind my grumpy daughter." Herb Rhodes mussed Randi's hair. "She'll catch Founders' Day fever soon. And I gotta say, the town's looking better than ever. You picked the perfect shade of yellow for the ice cream parlor, Betty. Looks like you've got some nice new tables in there, too."

"Glad you like them." Mrs. Prufrock beamed. "The renovations took every last dime that I had. Not that I'm complaining. I don't think there's a savings account in Deer Creek that wasn't drained to spruce up the town. Only one who didn't chip in was Angus McCarthy," she said with a bitter nod at the ramshackle bait shop across the square. "But that's to be expected, I suppose."

"Yep, if the mayor doesn't pull off this Founders' Day extravaganza, the whole town will go broke," the sheriff noted. "The tourists haven't been coming for years. I don't think I've issued more than twenty fishing licenses since summer began."

"But I know y'all didn't come to hear us moan and groan," Mrs. Prufrock told Randi and her dad. "Bet you'd rather have a scoop of my hand-churned chocolate chunk, wouldn'tcha? Come on inside." The Rhodeses followed as Mrs. Prufrock ambled through the doorway of her shop and slid behind the counter. Then she paused to give Randi a funny look. "You know, you sure have gotten pretty, Miranda Rhodes. Tell you what. I'll give you a second scoop on the house if you'll enter the festival's Miss Catfish Pageant. Someone's gotta keep that Amber-Grace Sutton from winning the title four years in a row."

"Yeah, um . . . no thanks," Randi replied rather tartly. She honestly couldn't imagine anything worse than getting all dolled up and prancing around on a stage in the center of town. Especially if it meant coming within fifty feet of Amber-Grace Sutton, the most obnoxious brat in east Tennessee.

"Oh well," Mrs. Prufrock replied with a sigh. "Suit yourself."

"It's not such a bad idea, Miranda," Randi's father jumped in. "Practicing for the pageant might help keep you busy for the next week."

"And what's going to keep *you* busy?" Randi asked dryly.

Before her dad had a chance to reply, his cell phone started to ring and he took it out. Randi caught a glimpse of the name on the display just before he stuffed the device back into his pocket. *Sullivan & Sutherland*, it read—the company that published the Glenn Street novels.

"Was that your editor?" Randi asked. "Why didn't you answer?"

"It's not a good time."

"Why's he calling, anyway?" Randi huffed. "Doesn't he know you retired? Or did you let him think that you moved down here so you could write about catfish?"

Herb Rhodes ran his fingers through his salt-and-pepper hair, shook his head, and turned his back to her. Randi knew that was his way of saying *Don't push it*.

"Here you go, Miranda," Mrs. Prufrock said, passing her a cone with two huge globs of chocolate chunk stacked on top. "I gave you an extra scoop anyway."

"Gee, thanks," Randi muttered. She wished the woman hadn't bothered. She'd gotten tons of free stuff after her mom died. Everyone had felt so sorry for poor motherless Miranda Rhodes. The last thing Randi wanted right now was Mrs. Prufrock's pity. She looked around for her dad and found him standing in front of the refrigerated display with a faraway look in his eyes. Randi had seen that look before. Her dad had worn the same expression for months after her mom got sick and he'd decided to quit writing. She *hated* that look.

Randi was about to offer an apology when her eyes were drawn to a flyer that someone had pinned to the parlor's bulletin board.

* * * LOST CAT * * *

FIFTY POUND

REWARD IF FOUND

Answers to the name PUMPKIN

A photo showed an obese orange tabby cat wearing a leash. Randi snatched the flyer. *A fifty-pound cat?* she thought. *Someone needs to lay off the cat treats and get rid of that leash.*

"Are y'all settling in okay?" Back at the counter, Mrs. Prufrock was handing her father a cone. "Is there anything we can do for the two of you?" the woman whispered just a little too loudly.

"Thank you, Betty. We're managing just fine."

"I was so sorry to hear about Olivia," said Mrs. Prufrock. "Cancer, wasn't it?"

"Yes," Herb confirmed.

Mrs. Prufrock shook her head. "Such a shame. She was a wonderful girl. And this must have been so hard on Miranda."

"She's adjusting." Herb looked eager to flee. He fished for money in his pockets and handed the woman a few crumpled bills.

"Hey, y'all?" Sheriff Ogle stuck her head through the door. "Just thought you might want to know that they've moved the monument. They're about to reveal the capsule."

"Great!" Randi's father sounded relieved. "We'll be right out!" He practically pushed Randi through the door and across the street to the edge of the park. Sheriff Ogle was already there, watching a young man set up a microphone stand in the park. He seemed to be the only citizen who'd been allowed onto the grass.

Randi took in the scene from the sidewalk. The backhoe that moved the monument had been driven away. The boulder itself sat off to one side, and the temporary fence circled whatever had lain beneath the rock. Ten Secret Service agents stood guard around the fence, and none of the townsfolk dared take a peek behind it. *So there really was something under the boulder,* Randi thought. Her eyes passed over what looked like a pulley system that was still lying on the grass. *The capsule must not be very big if they didn't bother to assemble the pulley.*

"So I'm guessing you know who the VIP's going to be?" Randi asked the sheriff.

The sheriff straightened her spine, and her voice took on an official tone. "The mayor will make the announcement as soon as the time capsule has been transferred to a secure location. Until then, I can't talk about it. It's OPB."

"It's *what*?" Randi's father asked.

"Official police business," Sheriff Ogle explained.

"Oh," Herb finally said with a wink to Randi.

"But see those men in the sunglasses?" the sheriff whispered. "Let's just say that they work for our VIP."

"They're Secret Service," Randi said.

"Shhh!" The sheriff glanced around nervously.

A gravelly voice called out from the sheriff's radio. "The goose is laying the golden egg! Need cover! Over!"

"Roger that." Sheriff Ogle spun around. "Gotta run. OPB!"

Handsome Mayor Cameron Landers stepped out of a car at the edge of the square. The sheriff met the mayor at the curb and escorted him across the park to the microphone stand.

"Good afternoon, everyone." Randi found it hard to believe Cameron Landers was the mayor of Deer Creek. At least ten years younger than her father, he looked like a mannequin from a ritzy Manhattan department store. He usually dressed like one, too. But this afternoon he'd paired black combat boots with his beige linen suit. He must have been worried that his fancy dress shoes would get covered in dirt. "I just want to take this opportunity to thank everyone for all the hard work you've done in preparation for Deer Creek's two hundredth birthday celebration."

Shop owners whistled and applauded from their doorways.

"In just a moment, you will witness history as Sheriff Ogle and I unveil the capsule that our honored guests have unearthed," the mayor said proudly. "It will then be transferred to the county jail for safekeeping. Next Sunday at noon, our legendary time capsule will be opened by the . . ."

Without warning, Angus McCarthy pushed a wheelbarrow across the sidewalk on the opposite side of the park and onto the grass. Toot McCarthy's only son and the owner of the Bait 'n' Tackle Shop, Angus was also known as the meanest man in town. The locals stepped aside when they saw him. They knew the old man wouldn't hesitate to run down anyone in his path. However, it was probably his cargo that worried them most. Inside McCarthy's wheelbarrow was a burlap sack. And inside that sack, *something* was wriggling.

The Secret Service agents blocked the wheelbarrow before it reached the monument. But that didn't stop Angus McCarthy. He simply untied his sack and let its contents take over. Out scuttled an agitated skunk. It slipped between two agents' legs and made a beeline for the mayor.

"This whole show stinks to high heaven!" McCarthy shouted. "What's going on behind that fence? You hiding something from the rest of us? Go get 'im, Rosebud! Show that fancy-pants college boy how we deal with trespassin' scoundrels!"

The Secret Service agents scrambled at the sight of the skunk. Two of them knocked over the fence in their rush to escape, exposing the hole that had been hidden behind it. Meanwhile, Rosebud chased the mayor around the small park. Just as Cameron Landers reached the farmers' market, he tripped over a clump of purple petunias and slid headfirst into the stand selling Sheriff Ogle's honey. Glass shattered, honey oozed, and while the mayor struggled to free himself from the sticky spillage, Rosebud lifted her tail and sprayed.

"Good girl!" Angus McCarthy cackled. "Now go get the rest of 'em!"

For the next few minutes, chaos reigned. Kids and adults screeched and scattered. Randi and her dad ducked inside Prufrock's for cover. The only one who seemed to have kept her cool was the sheriff. She grabbed an empty apple basket from the farmers' market and went after the odiferous critter. Randi had to admit that the sheriff was remarkably fast for someone shaped like a jelly bean. And when the skunk scrambled over a park bench, the sheriff leaped over it too. She caught the skunk just as it tried to slink past the fallen fence that surrounded the monument and trapped it beneath the upside-down basket.

Sheriff Ogle held the basket in place with one foot, and Randi saw her take a peek into the hole. When the sheriff finally sat down to catch her breath, a hundred people spilled out of the shops on the square. Most were applauding. One was shouting.

"Arrest Angus McCarthy, Sheriff! Arrest him!" the mayor demanded, his suit and boots dripping with honey. Everyone gathered around the sheriff held their noses as he drew near.

"Ain't illegal to own a skunk, Cameron," the sheriff panted. "Besides, I'm afraid we've got bigger problems than Angus's pets. You know where the time capsule is?"

"Of course I do!" the mayor exclaimed. "It's still down there in that hole. We never even got a chance to pull it out."

"Then take a look and tell me if you see the same thing I do. 'Cause it looks to me like our time capsule is *gone*." ☠

☠ Go to Appendix B to complete the Ninja Task!

CHAPTER FIVE

POI: Persons of Interest

A crowd gathered around the fence and peered down into empty hole behind it. It wasn't very deep—or very wide for that matter—but it was definitely *empty*.

"The capsule *is* gone!" Mayor Landers gasped in disbelief, swatting at the flies that swarmed his honey-coated suit. "What happened?"

One of the Secret Service agents stepped forward to offer an official report. "The monument was moved at precisely twelve hundred hours. My fellow agents and I were preparing to relocate the time capsule to the Deer Creek jail when a man released a skunk. The animal appeared to respond to the name Rosebud. Its owner was Caucasian, approximately sixty to sixty-five years of age. Six feet tall with graying—"

"I know what he looks like! He's standing right there!" The mayor pointed at Angus McCarthy. "What did you and your men do when he set the skunk loose?"

"We took cover, sir," the agent responded.

"And you?" The mayor wheeled around to face the sheriff.

"I apprehended the skunk," Sheriff Ogle answered. "That would be SOP, your honor."

"SOP?"

"Standard operating procedure, sir."

"Why wasn't anyone watching the capsule?" the mayor stormed.

"I suppose we never thought anyone would make off with it," the sheriff said.

Mrs. Prufrock shook her head as if she couldn't believe what had happened. "It can't be gone! The president is coming next week to open it!"

Randi glanced around at the crowd. Judging by their horrified expressions, they'd been counting on the president's visit and the attention it would bring to the town. Randi knew none of them could have been responsible. They all had too much to lose.

"Can we still have the time capsule opening ceremony?" someone asked.

"Without a time capsule? Looks like y'all are just gonna have to cancel Founders' Day," Angus McCarthy said, sounding anything but heartbroken. "I knew he was gonna find a way to call it off somehow. Y'all should have known better than to trust a fancy-pants college boy like Landers."

The crowd turned on him in an instant.

"This is your fault, you miserable old coot," Mrs. Prufrock

snapped. "That capsule would still be here if it wasn't for you and your skunk. In fact, now that I think of it, I bet *you* were the one who took it. I bet you planned all of this so the rest of us would go broke and lose our property the way you lost yours!"

"You saw what happened just now, and you think *I* was the one who took the durn capsule?" McCarthy countered.

An idea popped into Randi's head. She grabbed a pad and a pen from her backpack and quickly sketched out a diagram of the crime scene.

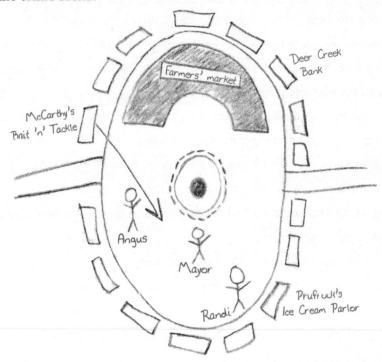

As she drew, she could sense the rage spreading through the crowd. And by her estimation, Angus *had* gotten close enough to steal the capsule during the confusion. Randi stopped and looked over at her dad. She could tell from the way he stood with his arms crossed that he didn't like where things were headed.

"Did anyone actually see Angus take the capsule?" he asked the angry mob. No one answered. "Well then, let's not convict him just yet. Sheriff Ogle hasn't even had a chance to investigate. And Angus might have a point. Perhaps we should consider postponing—"

"We're not all rich writers like you, Herb Rhodes," someone broke in. "Deer Creek needs visitors here spending money as quickly as possible! If you postpone the festival, you might as well foreclose on the whole town. And that's exactly what Angus McCarthy wants."

Mayor Landers raised his hands to quiet the crowd. "Folks, we're getting way ahead of ourselves. Rest assured, the Founders' Day Festival will take place as scheduled. I have the utmost faith in Sheriff Ogle, and there's no doubt in my mind that the time capsule will be recovered in the next seventy-two hours."

With that, he switched off the microphone and beckoned Sheriff Ogle over. A couple of Secret Service agents hovered nearby. Randi inched closer.

"That's all I can give you," she heard the mayor tell the sheriff. "Three days."

"I'll find it," Sheriff Ogle assured him, though she didn't sound confident.

"I hope so. Because otherwise, I'll have to convene an emergency town council meeting to consider postponing the festival. For goodness' sake, Mildred, how could you let this happen?"

"I'm sorry, Cam," the sheriff replied. "I . . ."

But the mayor had already turned to leave. A halo of flies were still flitting above him.

While Sheriff Ogle watched the mayor stomp off, Randi edged closer to the fence to get a better look at the empty hole.

Her father peered over her shoulder. "Well, what do you think?"

"It was there, all right." Randi pointed into the hole. It was a few feet deep and a couple of feet wide, and the bottom was lined with a sheet of black slate. On the surface of the slate was a clean, black square surrounded by two hundred years' worth of dust. "Looks like the capsule was just a small box. I'd say six by six inches."

"Too tiny for a treasure chest," Herb noted.

"That depends on the treasure."

"Excellent point," her father said, and Randi thought she detected a hint of pride in his voice. "Hey! Be careful!"

Randi ignored him while she scampered past the fallen fence. She squatted down to inspect the monument and the hole that had once held the capsule. The grass around the boulder had been flattened by the backhoe and at least three sets of shoes. There were three faint marks on one side of the rock. They appeared to match the crowbars that the agents had dropped. There was no evidence that anyone had ever tried to move the monument before.

Randi shrugged off her backpack and took out her camera. She moved quickly, expecting her dad to order her to stop, but he didn't say a word. She snapped pictures of the hole, the boulder, and the surrounding area.

"Where'd you learn how to investigate a crime scene?" Herb asked from above.

"From you," Randi replied.

"You're doing pretty well for a detective on her very first case."

"Who said it was my first?" Randi grumbled, but her dad didn't seem to hear.

"Find any clues yet?" he joked.

"Miranda Rhodes, you step away from that crime scene! You want to get me in hot water with the mayor?" It was Sheriff Ogle. She leaned in close as she helped Randi over the fence. "Well, did you?" she whispered conspiratorially.

"What?"

"Find any clues!"

"Nope," Randi said. "Though it looks to me like it was a crime of opportunity. Someone took advantage of the commotion to make off with the capsule. Judging by the size of the outline it left in the dust, the box might have been small enough to fit under a jacket."

"But who on earth would have taken it?" the sheriff moaned. "There hasn't been a single theft in Deer Creek since 2002! People round here don't even lock their doors."

"Then maybe you should start looking for people who aren't from around here," Randi said, scanning the crowd for suspicious-looking characters. Glenn Street always did the same thing, she remembered. Criminals were often drawn back to the scene of their crime.

Randi's eyes landed on a tall, skinny black boy. He was staring right back at her.

City boy, she thought. *No doubt about it. The latest sneakers and not a spot of dirt on them. A style of jeans that they sold at only the priciest stores in Brooklyn. A Red Sox cap with the brim bent just so. He must be from Boston. And judging by that scowl on his face, he'd love to still be there. So what's he doing down here?*

They held each other's gaze for a moment. Then the boy waded into what was left of the dispersing crowd and disappeared into the farmers' market on the other side of the square.

Randi started to hurry after him when her dad caught her by the arm.

"Where are you rushing off to?" he asked with a twinkle in his eye. "Following a lead?"

As usual, it was all a big joke to him. "I'm just going to hang out here a bit longer."

"Not too long," Herb Rhodes said. "Be home before dark. And stay out of trouble."

"Stay out of trouble? I wouldn't even know where to *find* it in this boring old town," Randi replied.

But as Randi made her way toward the farmers' market she could feel her heart pounding fast, like it did whenever she took on a new case. Along the way, she passed Angus McCarthy loading the skunk-filled apple basket into the back of his truck.

"I didn't take nothing!" the old man was grumbling.

We'll see about that, Randi thought as Angus got in his truck and drove off. *You're number one on my list of suspects. Expect a visit from me soon.*

When she reached the market, Randi stopped to survey the scene. The boy from Boston was long gone. Everyone else was a local, except for a woman working at the Guyton Orchards stand and an unfamiliar kid selling caramel-covered apples.

He was short and olive-toned, with unruly dark hair held back by a yellow martial arts belt that he was using as a headband. *The kid's a white belt if anything,* she thought. *Only a beginner would disrespect a belt that way.* Then the kid reached up to adjust the belt. Before he covered his ear, Randi noticed a piece of plastic tucked inside. *A hearing aid. That's why he wears his hair long. He's trying to hide it.*

The woman came over to deliver a bowlful of apples, all freshly washed and ready for dipping. She had black hair cut pixie short and a pretty face. Randi had assumed the woman was wearing long sleeves, but now she could see that both the lady's arms were covered in elaborate tattoos. *The boy's mom,* Randi quickly deduced. *And one thing's for sure. She didn't get those tattoos around here. Two more suspects for the list. Let's see what they have to say.*

Randi got in line for one of the caramel-covered apples. Just as she reached the table, she was shoved to one side. Amber-Grace Sutton, the town's spoiled-rotten Catfish Queen, had appeared out of nowhere with Stevie Rogers and his dim-witted posse.

"Nice manners, Sutton," Randi growled. "Now get to the back of the line."

"Did you just hear someone say something?" Amber-Grace asked Stevie.

Randi remembered the story about Stevie's ghostly encounter at Rock Hollow. Sure enough, his left arm was black-and-blue above the elbow.

"Four caramel apples. Three with nuts, one without," Stevie demanded.

The kid behind the table didn't budge. "You'll have to wait your turn."

Stevie wriggled his fingers as if using sign language. "Didn't you hear me, deaf boy? I told you to give me four of those apples."

"And *I* said you'll have to wait your turn."

"Never mind, Stevie," Amber-Grace chimed in sweetly. "Is that your mama with all the tattoos?" she asked the boy.

The kid narrowed his eyes and nodded.

"Then I think I just lost my appetite. I wouldn't eat anything that's been touched by that freak."

Randi couldn't let the insult pass. "Who are you calling a freak, Amber-Grace? You know why they make you Queen of the Catfish every year? 'Cause you look just like one."

Amber-Grace whipped around, tossing her long blond hair. "You're just jealous, Randi Rhodes, 'cause you're a redheaded Yankee scarecrow who'll never be pretty enough to be named queen of *anything*."

Randi sucked in her cheeks and made a fish face. The boy behind the counter chuckled. Even Stevie looked away to hide the involuntary grin that had spread across his face. Round one went to Randi.

"Don't just stand there, you idiot!" Amber-Grace swatted Stevie on his injured arm, and the bully took a menacing step toward Randi.

"You want a little more of what I gave you two years ago?" Randi asked as her hands formed two solid fists.

"Now, kids," said a deep voice behind them. "Can't we try to get along?"

Randi spun around to see a silver-haired gentleman in a pin-striped suit. It was Dean Sutton, Amber-Grace's father and owner of the Deer Creek Bank. "Amber-Grace, I thought you were supposed to be practicing for the pageant. How are you going to fit into that dress we bought you if you keep eating all those candied apples? Now run along, princess. I've got business here."

Amber-Grace and Randi held each other's gaze like sworn enemies. The Queen of the Catfish was the first to blink.

"Let's go," she snarled, and the bullies obediently followed behind her.

"Your mama around?" Mr. Sutton asked the kid behind the table. "Much obliged," he said when the boy mutely pointed to the spot where his mother stood frozen, staring at Mr. Sutton like she'd just seen a ghost.

"I hate Amber-Grace!" Randi stormed once the man was gone. "She thinks she runs this town just because her dad owns the bank! Ooh, and don't get me started on that oaf Stevie Rogers!" She stopped and took a breath. "Anyway, who are *you*?" It sounded tougher than she'd intended.

"Um, I'm . . . uh . . . Dario, Dario Cruz," the boy stammered. "But most people call me D.C."

"I'm Randi."

"I know," D.C. mumbled.

"*How?*" Randi asked suspiciously.

"That girl said it."

"Oh yeah." Randi let down her guard a little. "You from around here?"

"Nuh-uh, Nashville."

"And where were you ten minutes ago when the time capsule disappeared?"

"Right here dipping apples. My mom wouldn't let me leave work to watch. This is our stand. We bought the Guyton Orchard last fall."

"Then I live just down the road from you. We have the blue cottage at the end of Poplar Lane," Randi said. Now that the kid was no longer a suspect, she felt free to give him a grin. But he didn't even seem to notice. His attention was focused on something behind her. Randi glanced over her shoulder and saw D.C.'s mom talking to Mr. Sutton. The woman was clearly upset.

"That's just not enough time! Can you give us a little bit longer?" Randi heard her say.

"I'm sorry, Mrs. Cruz. One week is all I'm authorized to offer." Sutton flashed a toothy smile and set off toward the bank. "Oh, and don't forget to vote for Amber-Grace in the Miss Catfish Pageant!"

Mrs. Cruz hurried back to the apple stand, where a small line had formed behind Randi. D.C.'s mom shot him a frustrated look. "Stop dawdling, Dario. We've got customers!"

D.C. quickly put a chocolate-drizzled caramel apple into Randi's hand.

"No charge," he whispered. "Thanks for helping me out."

Randi took a bite. "My pleasure," she said without thinking. And that's when she realized it *had been.* ☠

☠ Go to Appendix C to complete the Ninja Task!

CHAPTER SIX

THE NINJA'S HIDEOUT

"Cracked the case yet?" Herb Rhodes joked as they sat down to a dinner of microwaved macaroni and cheese.

"I've got a few suspects," Randi replied.

Her father paused with a spoonful of neon-orange pasta poised an inch from his mouth. "You know I was kidding, right? The missing capsule case is starting to look like serious business, Miranda, and you're just a kid."

"And you're the one who dragged me down here to Dullsville. Do you really want me to die of boredom?"

"Miranda Jasmine Rhodes, what's gotten into you?"

"Nothing that wasn't in me before. Not that *you'd* have noticed."

Herb Rhodes sat back, crossed his arms, and gave his daughter a stern look. "Miranda Rhodes, you stay out of the way and let Sheriff Ogle do her job."

"If she does her job, I'll stay out of the way. But tell me this," Randi said, deftly changing the subject. "Why does everybody in Deer Creek seem to hate everyone else? Aren't little towns supposed to be friendly?"

"Who's not friendly?"

"Oh, I don't know. Why don't we start with the guy who set a skunk loose on the mayor."

"Angus?" Her father laughed. "He's just a cranky old man."

Randi toyed with her macaroni, but she couldn't bring herself to eat a bite. She missed her mother's home cooking. For the past year, she and her father had survived on canned soup and microwaved meals. "What's Angus McCarthy got against Mayor Landers?"

"Well, if you believe Mrs. Prufrock's gossip, Angus once accused the mayor of stealing something from him."

"What did he steal?"

Randi's dad swallowed a mouthful of pasta. "Dunno. Angus never said."

"I don't get it."

"It all happened seventeen or eighteen years ago, back when Cameron Landers was a teenager. He and some friends broke into that cabin over in Rock Hollow."

"The haunted one?"

"Yep. It used to belong to Angus's father."

"Toot the Treasure Hunter—the one who went missing."

"That's the man. Back then, Toot had been missing for only a couple of years, and Angus hadn't gotten around to packing up his father's stuff. I guess he kept hoping Toot would show up again. Then he caught Cameron Landers and some other boys looking for Toot's ghost and chased them away. He swore they'd stolen something from the old house. But he wouldn't say *what*."

"And that's why he set the skunk on the mayor? For something that happened a million years ago?"

"Oh, I'm sure Angus has had plenty of other complaints since then."

"So do you think he's the one who took the time capsule?"

"Anything's possible," her father said with a shrug. "I'm going to leave the investigating to the professionals."

Just when the conversation was about to get interesting, Randi thought.

"I can't believe that the man who created Glenn Street won't try to solve a real-life case. What's happened to you, Dad? Aren't you interested at all?"

"Oh, I'm *interested*. I plan to read about it in the Deer Creek paper. And you better promise me that's what you're going to do, too. Otherwise, I might not give you this. . . ."

He dipped his fingers into his shirt pocket and pulled out a pink postal slip.

"The postman left it in our box yesterday. It must have gotten tucked inside a catalog. I just found it this afternoon."

"Is that what I think it is?" Randi nearly leaped over the table. Her BPX5 had arrived!

~ ~ ~ ~

After dinner, Randi hopped on the rusty old Schwinn for a farewell ride. When she passed Guyton Orchard, a strange whim came over her, and she turned down the gravel driveway. A farmhouse sat in the distance, flanked by a big red barn. As she drew closer, she could see that time had not been kind to the buildings. Two of the house's windows were cracked, and its white paint was peeling. The barn was in even worse shape. A giant hole had rusted straight through the tin roof, exposing the wooden beams beneath it.

D.C. must not have heard the sound of Randi's bike riding over the gravel. He was out on the front porch of the house, practicing Tae Kwon Do. An old illustrated guide to blocks, kicks, and hand attacks was balanced on the swing in front of him. He still had the yellow belt tied around his head, but his wild black mane had broken free. Wisps of sweat-soaked hair were pasted around his face. Randi watched as D.C. popped off an impressive roundhouse kick, then doubled over with a racking cough. He grabbed an inhaler that was sitting on the porch railing. He took a puff but shoved the inhaler into his pocket the second he caught sight of Randi.

"Nice form," Randi told him, climbing off of her bike. "Where do you train?"

"Everywhere," D.C. replied. There was an unexpected edge to his voice.

"Where'd you get the book?" Randi pointed at the illustrated guide on the porch swing.

"It's my dad's. It *was*, anyway. We used to train together. He left the book behind for me when he moved. He's a brown belt now," D.C. bragged. "He doesn't need books anymore."

"You really a yellow belt?" Randi asked.

"What would *you* know about Tae Kwon Do?" D.C. smarted off.

Randi raised an eyebrow. "Enough to give you a lesson or two. For starters, you don't bend your knees enough. Your kicks will be more powerful if you're grounded before you strike. Here, I'll show you."

She climbed up the steps and gestured for the boy to move to the side. Then, in one swift motion, she executed a round-house kick. There wasn't a mirror, but she knew her form had been flawless.

"Not bad!" D.C. offered reluctantly, his face turning beet red. "What rank are you?"

Randi casually put her hands on her hips. "Black belt, first degree."

He nodded solemnly. "Then maybe you're worthy."

"Worthy of what?"

D.C. gave her a grin. "Wanna see something cool?"

He led Randi around the back of the house, where a flourishing apple orchard seemed to go on forever. The trees drooped with heavy, ripe fruit. D.C. plucked two ruby-red apples from a low-hanging branch and tossed one over his shoulder to Randi.

At the edge of the orchard sat an old toolshed. The rusted

frame of a bicycle leaned against one side. A few feet from the shed was a tall oak tree with a wooden platform built in its upper branches. D.C. snagged the rope that dangled from the tree and pointed up at a hoist fastened high above.

"Elevator to the crow's nest," he explained. "You can see everything for miles."

"Nice," Randi admitted, biting into her apple.

"You haven't seen anything yet," D.C. replied, opening the door to the shed.

Inside was hideout heaven. A small table sat at the center of the room. On it were mismatched plates and cups and a plastic bin filled with all sorts of snacks. Surrounding the table, ice chests doubled as chairs.

The walls of the shed were covered with martial arts posters. Most were of ninjas twisted like pretzels in gravity-defying, awe-inspiring poses. The two most prominent pictures showed Bruce Lee and Jackie Chan performing stunning feats of Kung Fu. Randi had to smile when she saw an ad for the BPX5 pinned to the back of the door. *Definitely friend material*, she thought before she remembered she didn't have time for friends anymore. She'd had lots of them once. Then her mother had died and Randi's detective duties had started keeping her busy. Over the past year, she'd said good-bye to every friend she'd ever had. Sometimes she missed a few of them, but it was easier to be alone than it was to feel pitied all the time.

"Impressive hideout," she said.

"I'm still working on it." D.C. cleared his throat nervously. "I'm thinking of starting a new club."

"Oh yeah? What kind?"

"A secret society of ninjas," D.C. explained.

Why does it have to be kid stuff? Randi thought, her heart sinking. *I'm too old for make-believe.* "Ninjas *are* a secret society."

D.C. didn't seem to know how to answer. After a long pause he added, "You can be in the club if you want. But first you gotta pass the test."

"You don't believe me? I may not be a ninja, but I'm a black belt in Tae Kwan Do. What do you want me to show you?" Randi asked, assuming a combat stance.

D.C. took a seat on one of the ice chests and grabbed a bag of chips from the snack box. "Who's stronger, Batman or Superman?"

"Easy," Randi answered as D.C. crunched his chips. "Superman. Batman needs gadgets. Although he does have a better car, Robin, and *Batgirl*."

D.C. nodded. "And who's faster, Jackie Chan or Bruce Lee?"

Randi chewed on her lip for a moment. "That's a tough one. They're both Kung Fu masters. Bruce Lee studied Wing Chun, the art of combat and self-defense, known for its speed. Jackie Chan is an acrobat and stuntman who trained under Lee. I'm gonna go with Bruce Lee, but I wouldn't want to meet Jackie Chan in a dark alley."

D.C. smiled. "That's it! You're in!"

He seemed so thrilled that Randi didn't have the heart to decline the offer. "Okay. Just make it a secret society of ninja *detectives*, and you've got a deal."

"That's even better!"

"Then it's official," Randi said, rolling her eyes. "Even though neither of us knows anything about Ninjitsu, I guess we are calling ourselves ninja detectives. So how many other members are there?"

"Right now, just two," D.C. admitted sheepishly. "Do you have any brothers or sisters who might want to join?"

"Nope," replied Randi.

"Yeah, me neither. It's just me and my mom."

"I live with my dad," Randi said, hoping she wouldn't have to explain. "And he's really overprotective, so I better start heading home. I promised I wouldn't be out too late."

"Okay." D.C. didn't hide his disappointment. "So when should we have our next meeting?"

Don't do it! Randi thought. *Glenn Street works alone! You can't have some kid with a hearing aid and an inhaler following you around! He's damaged goods. He'll just let you down.*

"Meet me in front of Prufrock's Ice Cream Parlor tomorrow morning at nine sharp," Randi said, ignoring her instincts. For some reason, she just couldn't help liking the kid.

"Your dad lets you eat ice cream for breakfast?" The boy sounded impressed.

Randi rolled her eyes. "We're not going to *eat*. We have to get started on our first big case, and I think the town gossip can help fill in a few details."

"Case?" D.C. asked.

"Of course! Who else in this dinky little town is going to be able to locate the time capsule?"

CHAPTER SEVEN

FAMILY FEUD

Randi peered through the window at the clock on the post office wall. It was 8:58. She checked her watch to make sure that the time was correct. *C'mon*, she thought. She was anxious to meet up with D.C. and get cracking on the case. At 8:59, the clerk rounded the corner and unlocked the door. *Finally!* Randi sighed in relief.

A few minutes later, she emerged from the building carrying a large parcel, which she strapped to the back of her bike. She'd asked her father's permission to spend her life savings on a brand-new bicycle. But he'd be expecting a standard model, and Randi knew exactly what he'd say when he saw the BPX5. *Miranda, you shouldn't squander your money on frivolous things.* That's what he'd told Randi when she'd spent last year's birthday money on a parabolic microphone kit. The same kit that had helped her identify the delivery van that was being used by a ring of coldhearted pigeon thieves. Of course, Herb Rhodes had never found out that Randi was the anonymous source who'd alerted the cops—and he still *tsk*ed whenever he laid eyes on the microphone's box.

Randi wheeled down Main Street toward Prufrock's. Deer Creek seemed quiet for a Monday. A few citizens went right on preparing for the president's visit, but their faces were grim, and a pall had fallen over the town square. She saw a Secret Service agent peeping into the dirty front window of McCarthy's Bait 'n' Tackle. *Looking for the capsule?* she thought. *Let's see which of us finds it first.*

The sound of a jackhammer suddenly filled the square. A small crew of men was replacing a patch of cracked sidewalk. The din made her homesick for noisy New York. She closed her eyes for a moment and tried to pretend she was back in Brooklyn, on her way to her favorite spy supply store.

Randi opened her eyes just in time to see a pair of Secret Service agents exiting a nearby café with steaming cups of hot coffee. Neither checked for traffic before they stepped out into the street. Randi steered hard to the right, brushing against one of the agents as she hopped the curb and . . . *WHAM!* She slammed into a trash can. Randi skidded across the concrete, her bike's pedal etching a long scratch into the sidewalk. The package on the back flew through the air and landed hard at the feet of the mysterious boy she'd seen the day before.

"Watch where you're going, kid!" one of the Secret Service men barked. All Randi could see was the mud-caked treads of their boots as the two agents stomped off across the park, leaving her sprawled facedown the sidewalk.

"Hey! You okay?" someone asked. The Boston kid offered Randi a hand. "You hurt?"

"I don't think so," Randi replied once she was back on her feet. But when she saw her package lying on the sidewalk, her heart nearly stopped. *Did anything break?* She used her house key to open the box. Then she tore through the wrapping and inspected the contents. A vial of footprint-casting powder had cracked. Fortunately, that appeared to be the extent of the damage. She gave a sigh of relief.

"Sorry, I should have said thanks . . . ," she began, but when she looked up, she saw that the boy was gone. She scanned the area and caught sight of him ducking down behind a parked car on the opposite side of the park. The two Secret Service agents had stopped a few feet away on the sidewalk. From Randi's vantage point, it almost looked like the Boston kid was *shadowing* them.

Just then a battered truck drove past and stopped in front of the bakery up the street. D.C. hopped out of the passenger's seat with a basket of apples. He was wearing faded jeans with a ratty T-shirt. The yellow belt was still wrapped around his head.

"Sorry I'm late! I'll be right there!" he shouted at Randi. "Just gotta make a quick delivery."

Randi locked up her bike and waited for her new sidekick, who already seemed to be slowing her down. The delivery was taking longer than D.C. had promised, and when she reached the bakery, Randi saw why. D.C. had been ambushed.

"Would ya look at Bruce Lee?" she heard Stevie Rogers say as she opened the door.

"You mean Bruce *Wee*," cackled one of his posse. "Get it? 'Cause he's so short."

"You know why Bruce *Wee's* belt is yellow and not black? It's 'cause he's so scared to fight that he pees in his pants."

"Oh yeah? Well, anyone who's earned a yellow belt wouldn't have any trouble kicking a bloated butt like yours," Randi informed Stevie.

The bullies spun around to face her. Stevie snarled, but Amber-Grace Sutton was all smiles.

"How did little deaf Dario earn a karate belt when he can't afford to take classes?" the girl sneered. "I hear his mom spent so much money on those tattoos that she can't even pay her mortgage."

It was the lowest of low blows.

"Because your dad won't give us enough time!" D.C. blurted, sounding dangerously close to tears.

"I was wrong about you, Amber-Grace," Randi said. "You're not a catfish. You're a *snake*."

Amber-Grace snickered. "I'd rather be a snake than a motherless Yankee. Let's go, guys. I gotta meet my *mom* at the boutique to have my dress hemmed for the pageant."

Somehow the girl had found Randi's weak spot, and it took

her a moment to recover. "Don't listen to them," she told D.C. once the bullies were gone. She just hoped she could follow her own advice.

"Amber-Grace was right, you know," D.C. said miserably. "I'm not a yellow belt. I'm not any belt. I've never taken a single class."

Randi shifted the large box in her arms. "Then I'd say you're a natural. If you want, I'll help you train. You could be really good if you stop thinking too much. In fact, here's your first lesson. Whenever you face a challenge, try to make your mind as still as water."

Sensei Daniel had told her that's what Bruce Lee always said. For a while, Randi had gotten quite good at it. But after her mom died, she'd forgotten how. Now D.C. was concentrating so hard on making his mind as still as water that his eyes were beginning to cross.

"Maybe we should practice later. We've got a case to solve, remember? And I'm supposed to be home for lunch. My dad made me promise. He's worried I'll get myself into trouble."

D.C. glanced down at her knee and frowned. "Looks like you already did. What happened to you? And what's in the box?"

For the first time, Randi noticed the bloody scrape on her leg. "I had a run-in with the Secret Service." Then she considered the box. She'd been dreaming about the BPX5 for over a week. After what she'd just heard in the bakery, though, she knew there was someone who could use it much more. "And *this* is a surprise for you!"

"For me?" D.C. asked. Before she could respond, Randi's attention was drawn away. Dean Sutton was leading a man in a business suit toward the bank on the opposite side of the square. Maybe it was the man's rigid posture or perfectly pressed suit that made him seem to be someone important. Trailing a few feet behind was the boy from Boston. She waved to get the kid's attention, but he was too busy watching his feet.

"Who's that?" D.C. asked.

"I was just going to ask you the same thing. When I fell off my bike, he gave me a hand."

"Never saw the kid before. That his dad with Mr. Sutton?"

"Must be, right?"

"Well, if he's friends with Mr. Sutton, he must be a jerk."

"A good detective never jumps to conclusions," Randi chided him. But she made a mental note to check the man out.

Mrs. Prufrock was wiping the tables when they entered the parlor.

"Miranda Rhodes and Dario Cruz," she said with a smile. "Did y'all see the sign outside? We don't start serving until eleven. I thought only one person in town ate ice cream for breakfast. And speak of the devil . . ."

Sheriff Ogle stepped into the shop, fanning her face wildly. "Woo! It's gonna be a scorcher," she said.

"Mildred, you're just in time. I was just about offer Miranda and Dario a free scoop of Cherry Dump Delight," said Mrs. Prufrock. "Don't suppose you'd like one?"

"Why, don't mind if I do."

"Thanks for the offer, ma'am, but we're actually here on business," Randi said with an official air.

Mrs. Prufrock looked bemused. "And what business is that?" Then her face burst into a mischievous grin. "Don't tell me . . . you've changed your mind about the Miss Catfish Pageant and you want a sponsor! You ready to give that horrible Sutton girl a run for her money?"

"No," Randi informed her. "This isn't about the pageant. We're looking for the time capsule."

"No need," the sheriff broke in. "I already know who took the time capsule and why. Just got to prove it."

"Then what on earth are you doing *here*?" Mrs. Prufrock demanded.

"I'm on my after-breakfast break, Betty. The investigation will recommence right after I finish my daily cone."

"So who do you think stole the capsule?" asked D.C.

"Yeah, who?" Randi chimed in.

"That information can only be shared on a NTKB. It's OPB." The sheriff took a lick off the cone Mrs. Prufrock had handed her before she explained. "That's *need to know basis* and . . ."

"Official police business," Randi finished for her.

"Oh, spare us the secrecy, Sheriff," Mrs. Prufrock huffed. "Everyone in town knows Angus McCarthy stole the capsule. What we *don't* know is why you haven't gone up there to take it right back."

"I guess *that* skunk's outta the bag." The sheriff sighed. "But you can't search someone's house just because people don't like 'im. You need PC. That's *probable cause*. Right now, I don't have enough proof for a search warrant."

Randi grabbed a notepad from her backpack. "Why are you so sure it was Mr. McCarthy?" she asked Mrs. Prufrock.

"Because Angus McCarthy wants this town to go under. He stole the capsule so we'd have to cancel the festival. He wants to force the rest of us to sell out the same way he did."

Sell out? How did Angus sell out? Randi thought. There wasn't enough time to ask.

"Or maybe Angus was after the treasure inside the time capsule," the sheriff added.

"I wish you'd stop talking about treasure, Mildred," Mrs. Prufrock clucked. "You're supposed to be the sheriff. You can't go around believing in silly old legends."

"Nothing silly 'bout treasure," the sheriff replied. "Toot always said there was enough hidden somewhere to put this town back on the map."

"And that's why folks laughed at him. Maybe if—"

"I'm sorry, but I'm missing something," Randi interrupted. "What's this treasure everyone keeps talking about?"

"Will it bore you to tears if I tell them the story?" the sheriff asked Mrs. Prufrock.

"Naw, go ahead," the other woman said with a sigh. "But the *short* version, if you don't mind."

The sheriff scarfed down her last bit of ice cream. "You've probably heard that Deer Creek was founded by three Irishmen. Liam Sutton, Jed McCarthy, and Sean Prufrock. Well, in 1813, they came to Tennessee to claim land, and all three of them wanted this beautiful valley. And they weren't the sort who liked to share. They fought each other that whole summer and into the fall.

"One afternoon, they were all down by the river when they heard a scream. Two Indian sisters had been canoeing downstream when their boat hit white water. One of the girls had fallen into the icy-cold river and the other had almost drowned when she jumped in to help her sister.

"No one knows which of the three founders acted first. But somehow the girls were saved. And as it turned out, their father was chief of a nearby tribe. When the founders returned the girls to their people, the chief gave Sutton, McCarthy, and Prufrock a reward."

"The Deer Creek treasure," D.C. chimed in.

"So they say," Mrs. Prufrock grumbled.

"What was it?" Randi asked.

"No idea," the sheriff replied. "But it must have been something amazing, 'cause the founders spent so much time fighting over who deserved it most that none of them prepared for the winter. They ended up spending the season holed up in a cave. All three of them would have died if the Indians hadn't checked up on them. When spring finally came, they founded the town. And they named it after the two girls who'd been saved: Running Deer and Creek Walker."

"What happened to the treasure?" D.C. asked.

"Some folks say they spent it. Some folks, like Betty here, claim there was never a treasure to begin with. And some think they buried it under that monument in the middle of town."

"Why would they do *that*?" Randi asked.

"Way I always heard it, when the founders couldn't decide how to split it up, they figured whoever's family lasted the longest would be the one that deserved it."

"See what I mean?" Mrs. Prufrock scoffed. "It's just a silly old story. Hard to believe it's still causing so much trouble today."

"It's a silly old legend that got the President of the United States to come to Deer Creek," the sheriff pointed out. "You think he'd have been so willing to open that capsule if he hadn't heard the founders' story?"

"Everyone loves that story, Mildred. But you and Toot are the only ones who were ever gullible enough to believe it."

"So Toot the Treasure Hunter was looking for whatever the Indian chief gave Deer Creek's three founders?" Randi asked.

"Yep," the sheriff replied. "When the McCarthys started

having money problems, he set out to search for it."

"Toot was just as crazy as his son, Angus," Mrs. Prufrock added. "Every morning, the old man would put on that safari hat and head off into the woods. If he'd just gotten a *job*, he mighta earned a little money and saved his son from having to sell out."

"Sell out? What exactly did Angus McCarthy sell?" Randi asked.

"He sold Toot's old cabin. Mayor Landers offered to buy up the house and the land behind it. But that miserable coot said he wouldn't part with the land for any price. Then he went and sold the first house ever built in Deer Creek to a Yankee."

"And then he stole the time capsule because he wanted the rest of you to be ruined, too?" Randi asked.

"Not all of us are going to be ruined," Mrs. Prufrock said. She was glaring out the window of her shop.

From where Randi stood, she could see Mr. Sutton and the man in the business suit through the window.

"Dean Sutton will be *just* fine. That vulture's gonna swoop down and pick this whole town clean," Mrs. Prufrock said.

"Who's the man with Mr. Sutton?" D.C. asked.

"That there's the Yankee who bought Rock Holler."

CHAPTER EIGHT

ROCK HOLLOW

"I think we've got a new suspect," Randi confided once she and D.C. were alone.

"Who?" D.C. asked. "Everyone seems pretty sure that Angus McCarthy stole the capsule."

"He's not the only one who has a reason for hoping the festival gets canceled. Who gets the town if the tourists never come and Deer Creek goes broke? Dean Sutton and his bank!"

"Mr. Sutton's after our orchard, too," D.C. admitted. "My mom's been scrimping and saving, but we can't pay the bills. We've been eating apples practically three meals a day, and it still hasn't done any good. Looks like Sutton's going to get what he's after."

"Not if we find that capsule!"

D.C. gave her a sad smile. "This has been fun, but you know we're just kids, right?"

"No, we're not! We're ninja detectives! And the stuff I've got in this box will prove it!"

Randi set the box down on the sidewalk and took out one item at a time. "Foot-print casting powder. Fingerprint-dusting powder. Luminol and a lumalight. Police radios. And . . ." She pulled out the folding bicycle and held it out to D.C. "A present for you."

D.C.'s jaw dropped. "Is that the . . ."

"BPX5? It sure is. One cubic foot in volume, with six-inch rubber tires and aluminum hubcaps."

"And you're giving it to *me*?"

Randi shrugged as if it were no big deal. "I just bought the kit for the detective stuff. I already have a bike." She pointed down the sidewalk at the rusty old Schwinn that was chained to the bike rack.

"No. I can't . . . ," D.C. started. "I mean my mom . . ."

"Geez, D.C., do you tell your mom everything? If she asks any questions, just say it's a loaner. Now unfold that bike and follow me!"

They raced out of town and toward the mountains. Randi had hoped some fun would help D.C. forget his worries. Now she could hardly remember her own.

"This is so *sweet!*" D.C. yelled, pedaling like mad. The small bicycle fit him perfectly, and he handled it with ease.

Randi slowed for a moment to point at a white clapboard dwelling at the side of the road. It must have been a lovely old house once, but several of its shutters were now hanging from their hinges, and the garden in front had gone to seed. "Isn't that where Angus McCarthy lives?" she shouted back at her friend.

D.C.'s eyes widened, and he nearly ran off the asphalt and into some bushes. That's when Randi saw Angus standing at the end of his drive, checking his mailbox.

"Stop spying on me! I ain't got nothing!" the old man bellowed, slamming the mailbox and shuffling back toward his house. Randi heard a dog bark and the front door slam. Then a massive Rottweiler came barreling down the drive. For a moment, Randi was sure that McCarthy had set the dog loose on them. But the mutt raced right past the bikes. Up ahead, an enormous orange blob disappeared around a curve in the road, with McCarthy's dog hot on its trail. Something about the blob seemed awfully familiar. . . .

"It's Pumpkin, the fifty-pound cat!" Randi shouted. "Quick, D.C. We can claim the reward!"

But as soon as they got around the bend in the road, the cat was gone. A muddy drive sloped off to the left. Randi hopped off her bike. There were several sets of prints in the soft earth. Most looked like dog prints. A few could have been possum or raccoon. Then she noticed a set with a long line drawn between them and remembered the photo on the flyer in Prufrock's. The cat in the picture had been wearing a leash.

"Pumpkin went down this road," she told D.C. "Let's go!"

But D.C. seemed to have lost his enthusiasm. "You've got to be kidding," he said. "That's Rock Hollow. It's haunted!"

"We're ninja detectives," Randi reminded him. "We aren't afraid of ghosts."

She climbed back on her bike and headed off down the road to Rock Hollow. D.C. hesitated. Then she heard him jump on the BPX5 and come after her. It was a sunny afternoon, but tall trees cast shadows in the heavily wooded dell. Branches almost seemed to reach out for Randi and D.C. as they passed. Needle-sharp brambles and poison ivy grew by the side of the road.

At the end of the drive sat Toot McCarthy's old cabin. Its wood-shingled walls were gray with age, and the rock chimney on top of its steep-sloped roof looked ready to topple. Randi and D.C. stopped a few yards from the house. D.C. pulled his inhaler out of his jeans pocket and sheepishly took a puff.

"Any sign of Pumpkin?" he wheezed.

Randi spotted a set of paw prints in the damp soil by the house. She left her bike in the drive and went to investigate. "Yep. These are definitely his paw prints." Randi squatted down. "Hmm, very interesting. Come look at this."

D.C. crouched down beside her. "What do you see?"

"These are his front paws," Randi said, pointing to two prints. "Now look at the hind ones. See any difference?"

"I see it! Pumpkin must have an extra toe on his front paws!"

"That's right. I'm going to go ahead and make a cast of these prints just in case Pumpkin gets away from us. At least we'll be able to give the owners proof that he's alive and well. They must be worried sick."

"How long will it take?" D.C. asked. Randi could tell he was itching to get out of spooky Rock Hollow.

"Just a few minutes," Randi replied, rummaging through her kit for casting powder.

"What are we going to do while we wait?"

"Keep searching for Pumpkin!"

"I'm not setting foot in that cabin," D.C. insisted.

"Then what's back there?" At the edge of the woods, a well-worn path headed up the side of the mountain.

"Snakes. Poison ivy. Bears. Caves."

"That's right! There are supposed to be caves in the mountain above Rock Hollow. Let's go have a look!"

"This isn't our property, Randi. We're already trespassing."

"Well, we're not the only ones. Looks like a lot of people have been through here lately." She pointed to boot marks on the trail. "In fact, forget the casting powder. I'll just snap a picture of Pumpkin's print, and we won't have to wait to explore."

Randi pulled out her phone to take a picture and yelped the second she saw the screen.

D.C. almost jumped out of his skin. "What's is it?" he wheezed, fumbling for his inhaler.

"Is it really twelve thirty?" Randi asked. The phone's message light was blinking, but there was no reception in the Hollow. "I think my dad called. He's gonna kill me. I was supposed to be home by noon!"

"You're only half an hour late."

Suddenly they heard a crash inside house, followed by the wail of an angry cat.

D.C.'s face went white. He jumped on the BPX5 and spun its wheels around. "It's the ghost!" he shrieked and nearly ran Randi down.

Randi's heart was pounding so hard that she was afraid it might break right out of her chest. *Stay cool,* she thought. *It's just Pumpkin.*

She turned to face the rundown house, and her blood turned to ice. A figure was watching her from one of the windows!

Randi raced away from the cabin. D.C. was waiting for her when she reached the main road.

"I saw him!" Randi cried as she gasped for air. "I saw Toot!" ☠

☠ Go to Appendix D to complete the Ninja Task!

CHAPTER NINE

THE AMBUSH

It was almost one o'clock when Randi raced toward her house on Poplar Lane, still searching for an excuse for being so late for lunch. She skidded to a stop by the side of the house and snapped the Schwinn's kickstand into place. When she rounded the corner, she was startled to find a woman sitting on the front-porch swing. She and Randi's father were sipping lemonade and munching on a plate of Lorna Doones.

The woman looked like she might be in her early sixties. She was petite, with long gray hair, which she wore in a loose ponytail tied at the nape of her neck. On closer inspection she seemed even younger because her face had no wrinkles.

"There she is!" Randi had expected her father to be furious. Instead he sounded nervous. "Miranda, you remember Mei-Ling, don't you?"

"Is that really Randi?" the woman said with a faint accent. "It's amazing! You were right, Herb. She looks just like her mother!"

Suddenly Randi was too angry to speak.

"Mei-Ling has been in Hong Kong visiting family," Herb said. "But now that she's back, she'll be staying with us. Taking care of . . . the house and whatnot."

"Where's she supposed to sleep?" Randi demanded. "Are you giving her my room?"

"Of course not. I cleaned out the guest room this morning."

"We don't have a . . . ," she started to say. "Wait—are you talking about the *studio*?"

"You got it," he said a little too cheerfully. "So why don't you go ahead and show Mei-Ling up to her room?"

The air grew thick, and a dry lump swelled in Randi's throat. She brushed past her father, avoiding his eyes. *This has got to be the biggest insult of all time. While I was out investigating crimes and spotting ghosts, my father went and hired a nanny.*

With Mei-Ling in tow, Randi stomped through the house and up the stairs to the room that had once been her mother's studio. Now it was just a place for strangers to sleep.

"This is . . . um . . . it," Randi stammered and backed out of the doorway.

She'd been avoiding the studio since she and her father had returned to Deer Creek. Every time Randi passed by the door, she'd tried to imagine that her mother was in there, painting by the window, where the light was best. The thought gave

Randi a few seconds of happiness every day. Now she'd even lost that. The last time Randi had set foot in the studio, it had been filled with her mother's art. She remembered countless canvases covered with beautiful blooms. Painting flowers had been her mother's specialty. Randi inhaled deeply, hoping she might catch a whiff of the verbena perfume her mother always wore. But there was not a single trace of her mother still left in the room.

Randi fled before Mei-Ling could see her tears. She dashed down the stairs and flung open the door to the cellar. And just as she'd suspected, that's where her father had put them. Her mom's paintings were piled against the wall like a bunch of unwanted junk.

She found her dad tidying up in the kitchen. "You threw her stuff in the cellar?" Randi shouted.

"You mean the paintings? The cellar was the only place to store them. Mei-Ling needed a room."

"Why is she even here? I thought we agreed that I didn't need anyone looking after me," Randi growled.

"You might not, but I certainly do," Herb joked, trying his best to lighten the mood. "Besides, Mei-Ling's not a babysitter. I told you she'd be looking after the house and whatnot."

"I know you think I'm just a dumb kid. It wouldn't take a mastermind to figure out I'm the 'whatnot' in this equation."

"Miranda, I don't know why you're so upset. We need

someone around to help take care of things. You know I'm barely able to boil an egg, and a child your age should have home-cooked meals."

"A *child* my age?"

"You know what I'm trying to say," Herb countered.

"The only thing I know is that you don't know *me* at all. You never have. Back when I was little, you were too busy flying around the world, going from one book tour to the next. Even after Mom died, you couldn't be bothered getting to know me. If you'd tried, you'd see that I'm not the same kid I was a year ago. So why don't you have a seat, Dad, 'cause I think it's time you found out who I *really* am."

Just then, Mei-Ling appeared carrying a small bag of spices and dried peppers. As she placed them on the counter, she offered Randi a smile.

"Secret ingredients for my special dish. I brought them back from Hong Kong. You like dumplings, Miranda? I make a hundred kinds of dumplings. I'll make catfish dumplings, just for you."

Randi glared at Herb. They had been talking about her. How else would the woman know that dumplings were her favorite food?

"Not hungry," Randi said, and stormed out.

By the time Randi reached Guyton Orchards, she was hot, exhausted, and out of breath. The wagon she'd latched to the back of her Schwinn was loaded with paintings. She never would have guessed that canvas and wood could be quite so heavy. Saving her mother's art would take at least three or four trips, and she'd barely had the energy for one.

"Halt! Who goes there?" D.C. shouted down from the crow's nest at the top of the oak tree.

"Who do you think?" she called up to him. "You got any other friends?"

He shimmied down the tree using the rope elevator.

"What's all that?" he asked.

"I brought some more stuff for the hideout."

D.C. eagerly examined the wagon's cargo. Then he stopped and frowned. "Flower paintings? You brought a bunch of girl junk?"

Randi's tough exterior crumbled. She could feel the hot tears flowing down her cheeks.

"I'm sorry!" D.C. yelped. "Don't cry! I didn't mean it! I like flowers, too!"

"They're my mom's. She painted them. And my dad just tossed them into the cellar. He wants to erase her from our lives. He doesn't care. You know, he didn't even cry after she died. Not once. I hate him!"

D.C. looked shocked. "No, you don't," he insisted.

Randi angrily brushed away the tears. "Yes, I *do*. He packed my mom's stuff away to make room for *her*."

"Who?"

"The nanny! My dad hired a stinking *nanny* because he thinks I'm a little kid."

"There's nothing wrong with being a kid, Randi. Sometimes it's a whole lotta fun."

"You mean it's a whole lot of fun being a *boy*. It's different for girls, you know. We get treated like we're fragile things that have to be watched and protected. You have no idea how lucky you are to be a boy."

"Can you repeat that?" D.C. asked sarcastically, tapping the hearing aid in his ear. "'Cause I'm pretty sure I didn't hear you right. You think I'm *lucky*? Just because I'm a *boy*?"

Randi choked back a sob. "You're not helping here, D.C."

"Sorry. It's just that no one ever called *me* lucky before. So who's this nanny your dad hired? Is she some horrible old witch or something?"

"No! That's the worst part! She's sweet and cool and she even said she'd make me dumplings!"

D.C. nodded as if he understood. "But she's not your mom."

Randi started to cry again and D.C. gave her a hug.

"It's okay," he said softly. "I miss my dad, too. He's still alive. He just has another family now. I don't see him that much anymore."

"That's terrible," Randi said, choking on her own tears.

"That's life," D.C. replied with a shrug. "Or so my mom says."

Randi used the collar of her T-shirt to dry her face. "Sorry to come over and cry like a baby."

"Sorry? We're friends. That's what I'm here for."

"Yeah, but . . ."

D.C. leaned in close as if he were about to tell her a secret. "You don't have to be tough all the time," he whispered.

CHAPTER TEN

THE FIFTY-POUND CAT

Once the paintings had been hung on the hideout's walls, Randi and D.C. stood back to admire the results of their labor.

"Ninjas, Kung Fu masters, and flowers. Not a bad combination," D.C. said, nudging one of the canvases to the left so it wouldn't cover his poster of Jackie Chan.

But looking at the paintings just made Randi feel worse. They wouldn't be hanging in a toolshed on the edge of an apple orchard if her mother weren't gone for good. Randi felt the tears welling up in her eyes again.

Get it together, she ordered herself. *Glenn Street doesn't get sad. She gets even. Show Herb Rhodes who he's dealing with. You're not a crybaby kid! You don't need a nanny looking after you! You're the Brooklyn vigilante. You fight crime and protect the innocent!*

"We've got to go back," she announced.

"Go back where?" D.C. asked.

"To get Pumpkin."

"What? Are you kidding? You want to go back to Rock Hollow after you saw a ghost there?"

"I'm not convinced that what I saw was a ghost," Randi said. "But I do know that cabin is dangerous, and Pumpkin's just an innocent old cat. He could get hurt in there!"

"Then let's call the owners and tell them we saw their cat go into Toot's house."

"And forfeit our reward?"

"Come on, Randi!"

She narrowed her eyes. "Are you a *real* ninja detective?" she demanded. "Or are you a kid playing make-believe?"

"I'm a ninja detective," D.C. insisted, sounding a bit hurt that she'd questioned his credentials.

"Then here's your chance to *prove* it," Randi challenged him. "You gave me *your* test. Now you have to pass *mine*."

In the shadowy late-afternoon light, the old house at Rock Hollow seemed to be waiting for them. The front door hung loosely on its hinges. The weeds around the building swayed in the breeze. Up close the house no longer looked haunted— just empty and sad.

The kids stopped their bikes at the end of the drive. Randi tucked a sprig of red curls behind an ear and went right to work unpacking her gear. "I'm going to take a cast of that paw print. I never got a chance to snap a picture when we were here earlier, and now the light's not so good. I don't know if a photo would capture the extra toe."

"Okay," D.C. said, his voice quivering. "But I don't wanna be here too long. This place creeps me out."

"Then come over here and I'll show you how to make your-self useful. I read about how to do this in—"

"One of your dad's books," D.C. said with a huff. "Just tell me what you want me to do."

"While I make a paste with the casting powder, I need you to collect some twigs," Randi said. "I'm going to build a dam around the prints to keep the paste from leaking out."

"Twigs?" D.C. surveyed the surrounding wilderness, an uneasy look on his face. "From the woods?"

"It'll speed things up."

D.C. sighed heavily and set off in search of twigs. A few minutes later he brought an armful over to Randi and dumped them at her feet. "What's next?"

"I made the paste and sprayed the prints with hair spray. It should harden and protect them. Now hand me a few of those twigs."

She built the dam around the prints and then checked to see that the hair spray had dried. "Give me a hand with this, will ya?" D.C grabbed one corner of the plastic bag filled with the casting-powder paste. Randi took the other. Together they poured the mix.

"It'll take about half an hour for it to become solid," Randi said. "Now let's have a look inside that cabin."

"NO!" D.C. almost shouted. "I mean, *why*? Even if Pumpkin was in there earlier this afternoon, he's gotta be long gone by now."

"Well, I'm going in," Randi announced. "You can stay out here by yourself if you want."

Being left alone in Rock Hollow didn't seem to appeal to D.C. "But what about the ghost?" he moaned. "What if Toot tries to rip off our arms like he did to Stevie Rogers?"

Randi felt herself shiver. "There's not a ghost on earth who's a match for a pair of ninja detectives!" she exclaimed, wishing she felt as brave as she sounded.

"Okay," D.C. reluctantly agreed. "But when we see that the cat's not in there, we leave. Deal?"

"Deal." Randi grinned and handed him a flashlight.

The front door of the cabin opened with a strained *creak*. Randi went in first. Inside, a few rays of sunlight managed to filter through dingy windows, but the place was eerily dark.

"Flashlight ready," Randi demanded.

D.C. clicked on his flashlight and directed its beam across the musty living area. Silky cobwebs covered everything and glistened in the light. A beetle emerged from a hole in the wall and scuttled across the floor into a forest of webs.

D.C. shuddered. "Well, I don't see any cat in here. Guess it's time to go."

Randi ignored the comment. She was busy bending down to examine a tuft of orange fur that had been snagged by a rusty nail protruding from one of the floorboards. "Look at this," she said, snapping a photo.

"What is it?"

"Cat hair." Randi collected the hairs with tweezers and folded them into a sandwich bag. "He's here. Now let's find out where Pumpkin is hiding."

She took a small spray bottle from her kit and lightly spritzed the floor. When she was done, she pulled out what appeared to be a long black wand.

"What's that?" D.C. asked.

"A lumalight. Body fluids like snot and urine give off a faint glow under a black light. And if you spray the area with luminol first, it will make any stains glow even brighter. Close the front door, would ya?"

When the room was totally dark, Randi flipped the black wand on. A faint swath of violet light shot across the floor. "Tell me what you see," she said.

In the darkness, paw prints glowed iridescent yellow. "They're everywhere!" D.C. marveled.

"Still think Pumpkin's not here?" Randi teased the boy. "What else do you see?"

D.C. pointed to a circular splotch in one corner of the room. It, too, glowed in the dark. "Is that what I think it is? *Ew.*"

"Yep. Looks like urine. But I don't think Pumpkin was just relieving himself. Looks like he might have been cornered. Cats sometimes spray when they're scared. Learned that one the hard way a few cases back." Randi walked over to the puddle and passed the wand over it. "Uhmm-hmm. It's definitely Pumpkin's. I can see where his leash dragged through the puddle."

"It's really dark in here, Randi. Can I open the door again?" D.C. asked with a tremor in his voice.

"Yeah, go ahead," Randi huffed. His scaredy-cat routine was starting to get on her nerves.

Randi heard the door open, and a dim ray of sunlight fell across the cabin's front room.

"Hey, I found something!" D.C. exclaimed, pointing down at the floor.

Sure enough, there were a few prints in the dust by the cabin's front window—and they didn't belong to Pumpkin.

"Good eye!" she congratulated D.C. "This is where I thought I saw Toot standing earlier today. But these are boot prints, and ghosts don't wear boots. Someone was inside the cabin!"

"Do you think it was the same person who scared Pumpkin and made him pee in the corner?"

"Maybe." Randi took out a magnifying glass and knelt down to get a closer look. "Do you see that? These footprints are crawling with tiny ants."

She pulled a roll of tape out of her backpack, cut three strips, and carefully connected them. Then Randi placed the tape over one of the prints, pressed, and then lifted the impression off the floor. The print had stuck to the tape, along with a few little ants.

"Wow!" D.C. exclaimed. "You really know what you're doing!"

"Thanks. Come on. Let's see what else we can find."

They ventured farther into the house. D.C. aimed his flashlight above his head to avoid walking face-first into cobwebs. The light captured tea rose–printed wallpaper, which was yellowed by time. In some areas, portions of the paper had peeled back, revealing another layer with a brownish color underneath. Large sections of the walls and floor had disintegrated, and all that remained was swollen and exposed wood.

"I don't care if this place is haunted or not," D.C. whispered. "It's really creepy. Maybe we should get going."

"Sure. Right after we check upstairs."

D.C. clutched her arm. "Do we have to?"

"Someone's been in the cabin," Randi reminded him. "They could have been looking for Pumpkin. If we want that reward, this might be our last chance to get it. It's now or never."

"I vote for never."

But he followed as Randi started up the creaky stairs. When they reached the second floor, they found themselves in a short hall with four doors.

"Which room should we check first?" D.C. asked.

Randi reached for a doorknob and threw open one of the doors. The room's windows were broken, and the floor was rotting away. Nothing.

The second room was empty too, aside from a bowl of

milk that had been placed in the center of the floor.

"Look!" D.C. exclaimed.

"How weird," Randi said. "That must be for the cat. Someone knows he's in here."

The third room's windows had been boarded over and the cramped little chamber was pitch black. The beam of Randi's flashlight passed over a large hole in one wall. Something inside sparkled.

"Did you see that?" D.C. gasped.

Randi rushed over and shined the flashlight directly into the hole. Pumpkin was curled up inside the rotten wall. His fur glittered like gold.

"What's that all over him?" D.C. asked. "It looks like he's been rolling around in gold dust! What if Pumpkin found the Deer Creek treasure? What if it's hidden somewhere inside this cabin?"

"You're jumping to conclusions again," Randi warned him. "We don't know that it's gold dust. And even if the cat did find a treasure, we don't know that it's here. Pumpkin's probably roamed the whole town in the last week. He's definitely gotten some exercise."

"Doesn't look like it helped much. He's still the size of a watermelon."

Randi bent down to pet the cat. "Haven't you heard that looks are deceiving? Pumpkin's plump, but he isn't all that fat. Feels to me like he's mostly fur. I bet he doesn't weigh more

than twenty pounds," she said, and Pumpkin purred in agreement. "Where have you been, you old rascal?" Randi asked.

"But if Pumpkin found the treasure, it could explain why someone was trying to catch him—" D.C. started to argue, and then stopped abruptly. A spine-tingling *creak* had just echoed throughout the house. "*Toot!*"

"Old houses make funny noises," Randi said, trying to sound brave.

She'd barely gotten the words out when they heard the sound of footsteps on the cabin's stairs.

D.C.'s eyes went wide with panic. Randi clamped her hand over his mouth before he could shriek. "Follow me." She grabbed Pumpkin with one arm and led D.C. to the hinged side of the door. If the door opened, they'd be hidden from view.

The kids held their breath. The footsteps became louder, closer. *KATHUMP . . . KATHUMP . . . KATHUMP . . . KATHUMP . . .* The floor creaked and groaned under the pressure. *KATHUMP . . . CREAK . . . KATHUMP . . . CREAK!* The footsteps stopped right outside the room where Randi and D.C. were hiding. Then a shadow stepped inside.

Randi needed both hands to keep hold of the cat. If the figure attacked, she wouldn't even be able to defend herself without letting Pumpkin go. She was trying to come up with a plan when D.C. leaped into action. Randi couldn't see well enough in the darkness to tell if he'd followed her advice and kept his knees bent. But the kick he delivered must have been powerful. The figure rocked backward and fell.

"AARGH!" it groaned.

"Nice work!" Randi cried. "He's down!"

"Let's get out of here!" D.C. yelled.

Randi and D.C. bolted down the stairs and out of the house.

They were only a few yards up the drive when Randi called out, "Wait! I can't run any more! I'm starting to think this cat really does weigh fifty pounds," she added, panting. "I'll hide here in the woods while you go for help."

"But the ghost!"

"If that was a *ghost*, you couldn't have kicked him," Randi noted. "Now take the phone out of my backpack. It gets reception at the end of the road. Run up there and call the sheriff."

"Are you nuts? Come with me!" D.C. urged her. "We'll go see the sheriff when we get to town."

"And let the person in the cabin escape? Don't you think the sheriff will want to know who was trespassing?'

"Aside from us?" D.C. asked.

"Go!" Randi ordered.

For the next ten minutes, Randi waited and watched. But no one emerged from Toot McCarthy's old cabin. She was starting to wonder if the person inside had been seriously injured by D.C.'s kick when Sheriff Ogle arrived, the siren on her police car wailing. She took out her gun, rushed to the cabin, and nudged the front door open with the toe of her shoe. Randi had to admit that the sheriff looked very professional from a distance. When she reappeared on the porch a few minutes later, Sheriff Ogle had put her gun back in its holster.

Randi stepped out of the woods and the sheriff shrieked.

"What were you doing back there, Miranda Rhodes?" she gasped with one hand over her heart. "You gave me the scare of a lifetime! I just came within a hair of soiling my uniform!"

"Sorry, Sheriff. Did you find the trespasser?" Randi asked. "Who was it?"

Sheriff Ogle shook her head. "There's no one inside the cabin. I checked every room."

"But that's not possible! I've been watching the whole time, and no one's come out."

The sheriff shrugged. "There's a reason people say the Holler is haunted. Now, you want to tell me what you and the Cruz boy were doing snooping around in Toot's cabin?"

"D.C. and I saw the missing cat sneak inside, so we went in to get him."

The sheriff reached out to pet the feline in Randi's arms. "Is that Pumpkin? I hardly recognized him. Poor thing looks like he needs a good bath. But little Molly Dunkin sure is gonna be glad to see him!"

"What's this stuff Pumpkin's got on him?" Randi asked. "It sparkles in the light. Do you think it might be gold?"

The sheriff laughed. "There's no gold in this part of the Smokies. That cat's covered in *mica*."

"Mica?"

"It's a shiny, flaky kind of mineral. Break open any rock and you'll find it. These hills are full of mica. They used to mine it round here. Now, why don't you ride back with me to town? Your friend's worried to death about you. And we can call the Dunkins and have them come to the station to pick up their cat."

When they arrived, the police station was empty except for D.C. and Mayor Landers. D.C. was sitting on a wooden bench, looking miserable, while the mayor paced the room.

"What are you doing here, Cameron?" the sheriff asked, but the mayor didn't bother to answer. He stomped straight up to Randi instead.

"I've got a good mind to call your parents, young lady," Cameron Landers announced. He wasn't very handsome when he was angry, Randi observed. His face was bright red, and a big blue vein on his forehead appeared to be throbbing.

"Now, Mayor, I don't think it will be necessary to get Miss Rhodes or Mr. Cruz in trouble this evening," Sheriff Ogle said, trying her best to soothe him.

"You two kids had no business trespassing on that land and wasting valuable police time!"

"They weren't doing anything the rest of us haven't done,"

Sheriff Ogle reminded the mayor. "I seem to recall that you and I went ghost hunting a few times back in the day."

"We weren't looking for the ghost, ma'am," D.C. said. "We were just trying to rescue the cat."

"This town's in serious trouble, and you call the sheriff out to Rock Hollow to help you rescue the Dunkin family's fat pet?" the mayor scoffed.

"Calm down, Cam," the sheriff ordered. Randi could tell that she was finally getting annoyed. "I was only out there for five minutes."

"Five minutes you could have spent searching for our capsule! I come down here to the station to give you important news and I find out you're hunting for lost cats."

"Well, I'm here now, aren't I? What's the big news?"

"I've just come from a town council meeting. It's been decided. If that capsule isn't recovered by midnight tomorrow, we're going to postpone the whole festival."

"But you said I'd have seventy-two hours! It's only been twenty-nine!"

"If you'd done your job, you wouldn't have needed *two* hours, Sheriff! Everyone knows where the capsule is. Now, if you don't go up to Angus's house and get it, I'll do it myself!"

The mayor stomped toward the door of the station, the soles of his books sticking a bit to the linoleum. He was halfway out the door when he turned and pointed a finger at Randi.

"And you two stay away from Rock Hollow! That whole

place is dangerous, and the last thing we need is to waste time rescuing a couple of grade-school troublemakers."

The door slammed shut and stayed closed for less than five seconds before a little girl rushed in.

"Pumpkin!" she screeched, lifting the massive cat out of Randi's arms.

"You must be Molly Dunkin," Randi noted.

"And this is her mother, Kate Dunkin," the sheriff said, nodding toward a blond woman who had followed Molly into the station.

"Thank you two so much for finding our cat!" Kate Dunkin said in a British accent. She leaned in closer to Randi and D.C. and spoke in a whisper. "I was a bit worried he was gone for good this time. My husband and I own the River View Hotel, and Pumpkin likes to hide out in our guests' cars. That's why we've had to keep him on the leash. But about a week ago he got loose again somehow. Where did you find him?"

"Rock Hollow."

Kate Dunkin shook her head in exasperation. "He must have hitched a ride in someone's vehicle. Pumpkin's too lazy to go that far on his own. Looks like he survived quite well in the wild, though. He's as fat as ever."

"He's pretty hefty, that's for sure," Randi said. Her back ached from holding him. "But he definitely doesn't weigh fifty pounds anymore."

Kate Dunkin gave Randi a funny look and then broke into

laughter. "He never weighed fifty pounds. Fifty pounds is the *reward* I offered for Pumpkin's return! Pounds are British money. I'm afraid I've lived in Tennessee for twenty-five years, but I still have a hard time thinking in dollars and cents. And I was so distressed the day Pumpkin disappeared. Here . . ." She handed a fifty-dollar bill to Randi and another to D.C. "I'm not sure what the exchange rate is these days. I think this should cover it, don't you?"

"Yeah!" D.C. shouted with glee.

Randi was speechless. She'd solved dozens of cases, but the money in her hand made it official. She was now a professional detective—and she couldn't *wait* to tell her dad. ☠

☠ Go to Appendix E to complete the Ninja Task!

CHAPTER ELEVEN

NOWHERE TO GO

Randi and D.C. stepped out of the police station and were nearly flattened by a kid riding a bike down the sidewalk at full speed.

"Sorry!" the boy called out, but he didn't stop. He seemed to be chasing a black SUV that had just disappeared around a corner, heading for the park at the center of town.

"That's the Boston kid. The one whose dad has been hanging out with Dean Sutton."

"Nice bike," D.C. noted, and Randi had to agree. The silver bicycle was brand-new, with thick, all-terrain wheels. "Where's he going?"

"No clue," Randi said. "Let's find out."

Randi and D.C. jumped on their own bikes and set off in pursuit. The chase ended when they turned a corner and found the street and sidewalk blocked by a crowd that had gathered outside the town hall. The citizens of Deer Creek had caught the mayor on the way back to his office.

"Is it true you're postponing the festival?" someone asked in disbelief.

"If the time capsule isn't found by midnight tomorrow, we don't have any choice," the mayor responded.

"But the bunting and the ribbons," someone else moaned. "What will we do with all of the bunting and the ribbons?"

"Bunting's the least of *my* problems," Betty Prufrock pointed out. "You postpone the festival and Dean Sutton's going to own my ice cream parlor in less than a week!"

"I'm sorry, Betty," Mayor Landers responded. "But I've done everything I can do. If you want to save the festival, I suggest you have a word with the sheriff and convince her to do her job!"

The mayor charged up the stairs and into the town hall, leaving an angry crowd in his wake. Without the festival, there would be no presidential visit. And that meant no tourists— and no money. The people of Deer Creek could lose their businesses, or worse, their homes.

"This isn't good," D.C. said. Randi knew from his expression that he was thinking about the apple orchard. "My mom's going to be pretty upset when she hears. I guess I better get home."

"Yeah, me too," Randi agreed. "I'll meet you at the hideout tomorrow at nine a.m."

"No, I'll come to your house this time," D.C. insisted. "I don't think my mom's gonna be in the mood for company."

Randi heard a faint wheeze when her friend inhaled, and she knew the stress must be aggravating his asthma. "Don't worry, D.C. You're not going to lose the orchard," she tried to assure him. "We'll find the time capsule before midnight tomorrow."

"I know," D.C. said with a smile, but Randi could see that he wasn't convinced.

By the time Randi arrived home, the dinner table had been set. *Uh-oh. Not a good sign.* She checked the clock on the kitchen stove and grimaced when she saw it was already six thirty. An angry voice was coming from her dad's office, and Randi crept down the hall to investigate.

"I've tried calling, but she won't answer the phone. This isn't like my daughter at all," Herb grumbled.

Oh yeah? thought Randi. *How would you know?*

"First she shows up an hour late for lunch; then she storms out and doesn't check in," Herb continued. "I just . . . I just don't know what's gotten into her, Mei-Ling."

"She's upset, Herb. Her whole life has changed. You should give her a little more time to get used to things," Mei-Ling replied. Randi was surprised to hear the woman pleading her case.

"What I *should* do is ground her," Herb Rhodes replied.

Randi had to think fast. She still had a bone or two to pick with her father, but nothing could get in the way of her investigation. The capsule had to be found or D.C.'s mom might lose the orchard. She couldn't afford to be grounded. Not tonight.

Give him what he wants. Be who he wants you to be—a silly, stupid little kid.

Randi tiptoed back to the front door and reentered the house, calling out cheerfully, "Dad! I'm home."

Here goes. She heard Herb stomping down the hall and held her breath. *Oh no*, Randi thought when her father walked into the kitchen with his armed folded across his chest. *Grounded for sure.*

"You know we have dinner at six o'clock. Where have you been, young lady?"

"Sorry, Dad. I should have checked in. It's just that D.C. and I were having so much fun that I lost track of time!" she explained in a bubbly voice. "We found that lost cat. You know the fat one whose picture is on those flyers around town?" She pulled the fifty-dollar bill out of her pocket and waved it in the air. "We got a reward and everything!"

Herb let his arms fall to his sides. "Who's D.C.?" he asked.

Whew. Randi exhaled. "He's a kid I met yesterday. His mom owns the Guyton Orchards now. We started a club!"

Herb cracked a smile. Since her mom died, he'd been after her to spend more time with kids her age, and she could tell he was pleased that she'd made a new friend. When he forced his smile into a frown, Randi knew what it meant. He wasn't mad anymore, but he didn't want her to think he was letting her off easy.

"Let's try to be more responsible from now on. Mei-Ling had to set the table tonight, and that's supposed to be one of your chores. If you want to be treated with respect, you first have to earn it. Understand?" he asked. Randi nodded humbly. "Okay then. Let's enjoy dinner. Mei-Ling made an amazing meal for us."

Crisis averted, Randi thought as Herb helped himself to catfish dumplings.

"You know," Herb said as he spooned sauce onto a dumpling, "I've been researching the Miss Catfish contest. I don't think it would be so terrible if you entered."

That's how you've been spending your time while I've been trying to save the town? Randi wanted to ask, but she knew better than to smart off. Even Mei-Ling was keeping her eyes glued to her own plate, making sure no one asked her to weigh in on the subject.

"Entering the pageant's too risky," Randi replied with a mouthful of dumpling.

"Risky?"

"What if I won? They'd make me wear that stupid catfish hat."

"It's a *crown,* honey," Herb corrected her.

"Whatever," Randi said. The subject was making it difficult to keep up her silly, stupid little kid routine. "I'm not entering a beauty pageant. I don't care if people think I'm pretty or not."

"It's not about being *pretty*," her dad argued. "The pageant's a tradition. It's a way of showing that you're proud of your town. Don't you want to show everyone that you're happy to call Deer Creek home?"

"I'm not," Randi mumbled as she pushed the food around on her plate.

"Excuse me?"

"I said I'll think about it, Dad."

"Really?" Herb asked hopefully.

"No," said Randi, deciding it was time to turn the tables. "By the way, did you ever call your editor back? Did you find out what he wanted?"

"Yes."

Randi's face lit up. "Really, Dad?"

"No," Herb admitted with a mischievous smile. "I haven't had time."

"Come on, Dad!" Randi said with a groan. "You've had plenty of time! Don't you think you should start writing again before you forget how to do it?"

"I'm too busy helping you settle in. Which is why I think the pageant—"

"There might not even be a pageant this year," Randi said, cutting him off. "The mayor's going to postpone the Founders' Day Festival if somebody doesn't find the capsule by midnight tomorrow."

Herb Rhodes stopped eating long enough to study his

daughter's face. "I hope you don't think you're going to be that somebody, Miranda. I don't want you poking around in places you don't belong. It's too dangerous." Herb picked up his fork and took a big bite. "By the way, these fish dumplings are delicious, Mei-Ling."

"It's all in the spices." Mei-Ling beamed. "How're your dumplings, Miranda?"

"Fine," replied Randi coolly. Herb shot her a stern look.

"Hey, Dad," said Randi. "I saw Sheriff Ogle this morning, and she told me the story about the founders' treasure. How come you never mentioned it before?"

"It's just a legend, hon. No one really believes it exists. Though I do remember searching for it a few times when I was about your age."

"D'you ever find anything?" asked Randi.

"Sure did. It was on one of those hunts that I discovered your mother," Herb said. "She was the greatest treasure of all." He stopped and cleared his throat. "Listen, kiddo. I know you're upset about what happened this afternoon, but I'm just trying to do what's best for our family. . . ."

"So hold a sec—you're saying that a person should do what's best for the group even if it might upset a person she loves. Is that right?"

Herb pondered the question. "There's an old saying: *The needs of the many outweigh the desires of the few.* I suppose I agree with that way of looking at things. Unless *the few* happen to be your parents." He ended with a hearty chuckle.

It's just a big joke to you, Randi thought. *Let's see if you're still laughing tomorrow.*

Randi woke at seven a.m. after a restless night of sleep. She'd tossed and turned for hours, worried she wouldn't be able to locate the time capsule by midnight. *What would Glenn Street do?* Randi rolled out of bed, and a bright yellow book on the night table caught her eye. It was a Mandarin Chinese dictionary with a note attached that read: *For mae mae. Love, Mei-Ling.* Randi was certain the book hadn't been there the night before, which meant Mei-Ling must have placed it on the table after Randi had fallen asleep. Had Mei-Ling checked on her like she was a baby? *She's got a lot of nerve,* Randi thought.

She opened her bedroom curtains to let the morning light in. On the front lawn below her window, a figure wearing black silk pajamas was practicing what looked like the ancient martial art of Tai Chi. Randi watched Mei-Ling's graceful movements. Her entire body seemed to flow from one position to the next, as if she were made of water.

Randi picked up the note Mei-Ling had left her during the night and stared at it again. *Mae mae.* What did it mean? Her curiosity got the best of her, and she flipped through the dictionary until she'd pieced together the phrase.

"Little sister," Randi whispered. She read the rest of the definition: *An affectionate term for a younger friend.* Then she tossed

the note into the wastebasket, slipped into a pair of jeans, and ran her fingers through her tangled curls.

After Randi's bed was made, her laundry separated, and the rest of her chores finished, she grabbed her fedora and hurried downstairs. The aroma of freshly brewed coffee, hot cocoa, and bacon filled the air. The house was cool and quiet except for the sounds of Mei-Ling preparing breakfast in the kitchen and her father typing away in his office.

She found Mei-Ling standing at the kitchen counter and cracking eggs into a bowl.

"*Ni hao*, Miranda. I'm making American-style hotcakes. You like hotcakes?"

"I saw you in the front yard. How long have you been doing Tai Chi?"

Mei-Ling continued mixing the pancake batter. "I learned in Hong Kong when I was young. I started training again a few years ago, when my husband died. It helped me with my grief. They say it is very good for the body and mind." She paused and looked up at Randi. "If you want, I could teach you."

"No thanks." Randi checked her watch. It was already eight forty-five. *Where's D.C.?* She pulled out a stool and sat at the island while Mei-Ling served her a plate of pancakes and some hot chocolate. Randi stared blankly into the cup and then hesitantly took a sip. It was warm and creamy and tasted a bit like cinnamon. Although Randi hated to admit it, the stuff was delicious. She settled in and took a bite of the pancakes.

Mei-Ling hummed and ladled more batter onto the griddle. A bleary-eyed Herb walked into the kitchen with an empty coffee mug. "Good morning," he said, half yawning as he pecked Randi on the forehead. "Mei-Ling."

"*Ni hao*, Herb. Would you like some breakfast?"

"Smells great," said Herb. "We haven't had pancakes in a while, have we, kiddo? Thanks, Mei-Ling. I'll take it back to the office."

Mei-Ling flipped a batch of pancakes with cheflike precision and placed them on a plate for Herb.

Randi saw the weariness in her father's every movement. His eyes were puffy with dark circles underneath, which made him look much older than forty. She could tell that he'd pulled an all-nighter.

"You look tired, Dad," she said, trying to sound casual. *Can he be writing again?* she thought.

"I've had a lot on my mind lately. Listen, sweetie, about yesterday. I should have told you I'd moved your mother's paintings to the cellar. But putting a few of her things in storage doesn't mean we'll lose her forever. Remember, she's the angel on our shoulders now. She'll always be with us."

"I know," said Randi, avoiding his eyes. Herb replied with a tweak of her nose, then retreated to his office.

Mei-Ling smiled and wiped down the kitchen counters. Randi watched him go and checked her watch again. *Still no sign of D.C. Has he given up? Is that why he's not here?*

She started for the door, but turned back to Mei-Ling, "Thanks for the pancakes," she mumbled quickly, and ran out.

Upstairs, Randi grabbed a book from the shelf in her bedroom. The previous day had been tough for D.C. As each hour ticked past, he and his mom got a little bit closer to losing their home. Randi could understand why someone might feel a bit hopeless in his situation. If D.C. needed a confidence boost, she knew just what to give him. With the book in one hand, she dug through her closet in search of the special *dobok* her mother had bought after Randi's first big competition. The martial arts uniform was hanging in the back behind her winter coats. Randi had outgrown it, but she hadn't had the heart to give it away. Now she dusted it off and wrapped it, along with the book, in brown paper. Then she crammed the bundle into her backpack and darted back down the stairs.

The sheriff's cruiser was parked in D.C.'s front yard when Randi rode up on her bike. D.C.'s mom stood barefoot at the top of the front steps with her thumbs tucked into the pockets of her ripped jeans. From a distance, she looked tough, like a rock star or a motorcycle chick. When Randi got closer, she could tell from the woman's bloodshot eyes that she'd been crying.

Dean Sutton waited by the cruiser as the sheriff delivered an orange piece of paper to D.C.'s mother.

"You said a week!" Mrs. Cruz yelled at Sutton. She snatched the paper out of the sheriff's hands.

"Now that it looks certain the festival will be postponed, I'm afraid that you aren't going to be able to make the back payments," the banker informed her.

"The festival hasn't been canceled yet," said Mrs. Cruz. "We still have until midnight, right, Sheriff?"

"That's right, ma'am," Sheriff Ogle confirmed, shooting Dean Sutton a disgusted look.

"Please try to understand the bank's position, Mrs. Cruz. We've done just about all we can do. Our hands are tied," Sutton said, almost sounding sincere. "However, given the circumstances, the bank is prepared to give you until the end of the week to vacate the premises."

"But we don't have anywhere to go!" cried Mrs. Cruz. She plopped down on the front steps, tears streaming down her face.

Randi spotted D.C. crouching behind the porch. When their eyes met, he took off through the orchard. She chased after him on her bike.

When she caught up with him, D.C. was standing at the base of the lookout tree, taking his frustration out on a fallen branch but failing miserably at his attempt to break it. He angrily kicked the limb aside and took a deep puff on his inhaler.

"It's gonna be okay," Randi tried to assure him.

"I don't wanna talk about it." He gave the branch another kick.

"Remember—you've gotta become like water," Randi said.

"What?" D.C. asked, annoyed.

"You're thinking too much about breaking the branch. Empty your mind and your moves will flow like water."

"That's stupid," snapped D.C.

"I wasn't the one who came up with it," said Randi, setting the package at his feet. "Look, the way I see it, we *have* to find that time capsule now."

"Sure," said D.C. sarcastically.

"If we find it, the president will come and the mayor won't cancel the festival. You won't have to move. And we can be best friends forever."

"We're not going to find it, Randi! We're just a couple of dumb kids."

"That's exactly what you're acting like. A dumb kid." Randi headed to the hideout door. "If you wanna help, I'll be inside reviewing the case. And just so you know, Bruce Lee was never a quitter."

Peeping through a hole in the hideout's wall, she saw D.C. stare down at the package she'd left at his feet. Then he picked it up and ripped off the wrapping paper. Inside was the *dobok*, a black belt, and a book called *The Warrior Within: The Philosophies of Bruce Lee*. Randi giggled when she saw D.C.'s jaw drop. He flipped through the book and stopped at a page she'd marked. She remembered the words she'd highlighted. *Empty your mind. Be formless. Shapeless. Like water.*

A newly inspired D.C. walked into the hideout and got to

work. While Randi pinned a large sheet of paper to one wall, he unloaded her detective kit.

"So what's next?" he asked.

Randi smiled and took a Magic Marker out of her backpack and began to make notes. "We know the time capsule is missing. We know it was taken the day the monument was moved. Angus McCarthy and Dean Sutton are our two prime suspects. McCarthy's motive is revenge. Sutton's motive is greed."

"You got that one right," D.C. said with an angry sneer.

"And there might be a link between our two suspects. Angus McCarthy's mad that he had to sell his dad's old cabin at Rock Hollow. The Boston businessman who bought the cabin is in town, and we've seen him in the company of Dean Sutton."

"Do you think McCarthy and Sutton are working together to ruin Deer Creek?" D.C. asked.

"I don't know," Randi admitted. "All I know is that everything seems to be connected to Rock Hollow. The capsule disappeared when Angus McCarthy set a skunk loose on the mayor. You know why Angus McCarthy hates Mayor Landers? My dad said Angus once accused the mayor of stealing something out of Toot's cabin . . . in *Rock Hollow*."

"And there have definitely been a few people snooping around up there lately."

"And at least one person pretending to be a ghost."

Randi sat down on the floor and stared up at the notes she'd made.

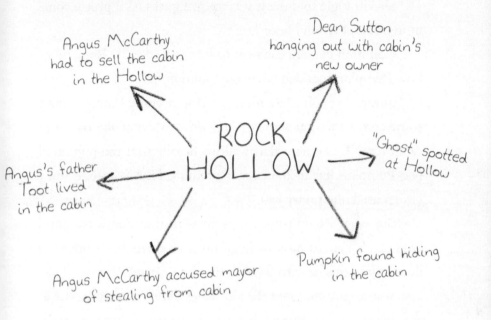

Angus McCarthy had to sell the cabin in the Hollow

Dean Sutton hanging out with cabin's new owner

ROCK HOLLOW

"Ghost" spotted at Hollow

Angus's father Toot lived in the cabin

Angus McCarthy accused mayor of stealing from cabin

Pumpkin found hiding in the cabin

"I think we should have another look at the evidence we collected at Rock Hollow the other day."

D.C. dragged a box out from under the hideout's table. He passed the evidence to Randi piece by piece. A plastic Baggie filled with cat hair. The tape they'd used to lift the impression left by the *ghost's* boots. And the cast of a paw print made by a fat feline with six toes.

"Hey, how 'bout that!" D.C. said, grabbing a magnifying glass for a closer look at the cast. He passed the glass to Randi. Glittery, brassy specks were embedded in the plaster. "It's the same stuff Pumpkin had all over his fur when we found him."

"Sheriff Ogle told me it was mica. I guess it's a pretty common mineral around here."

"Common enough for a cat to be covered in it? Remember how Pumpkin sparkled when we found him?"

"Interesting point," Randi said. "Where could Pumpkin have come across that much mica? And why was someone trying to catch him? Remember that wail we heard? And the puddle of pee Pumpkin left in the corner of the cabin? Someone must have scared him pretty bad."

"But what would someone want with that dumb old cat?" D.C. said, his enthusiasm beginning to dwindle. "And what does any of this have to do with the time capsule?"

"You've got me," said Randi. "Rock Hollow seems to be at the center of the mystery, but I feel like we're missing something important."

"I say we check out Dean Sutton," D.C. said. "Why is he here at my house with an eviction notice before the official deadline? How come he's so sure that the time capsule won't be found? He knows something—I'd bet anything on it. The question is what?"

"That's what we have to find out. Here's the plan." ☠

☠ Go to Appendix F to complete the Ninja Task!

CHAPTER TWELVE

LAST RESORT

Randi and D.C. slipped inside the Deer Creek Bank and scanned the lobby. Like most businesses in town, the bank was practically empty. And if the time capsule wasn't recovered by midnight, the other businesses in Deer Creek were likely to stay that way.

"Three tellers. Two older ladies counting cash. One younger teller waiting on customers," Randi observed through clenched teeth.

D.C. leaned in to Randi and whispered, "What if this doesn't work?"

"It will," she assured him. "You keep that young teller busy. I'll look for Sutton's office and see if there's a way to slip inside."

The pretty, young teller waved D.C. over.

Randi whispered, "Implementing Phase One," as they crossed the room.

While D.C. passed a plastic bag filled with loose change to the woman, Randi took in the lobby and its furnishings. She'd never set foot in the bank for fear of running into Dean Sutton's daughter Amber-Grace. The room's low ceiling made her feel claustrophobic. It was decorated in garish reds, accented in yellows, and completely overfurnished. *Just like Amber-Grace—small, stuffed, and heavily painted.*

Randi chuckled to herself. Then she instantly stopped when she spied Dean Sutton sitting behind the desk in a glass-walled office nearby. The Boston businessman was seated across from him. Randi tried to get D.C.'s attention, but he was too busy making eyes at the teller.

"Ten, twenty, twenty-five, twenty-five dollars and thirteen cents," the pretty blonde counted, placing the money in D.C.'s hand. "You sure had a lot of change! Is there anything else you need, cutie?"

"No thanks," he replied sheepishly.

"That's a lot of money for a little boy." The teller reached down and tousled his dark hair. "You're so adorable! How old are you?"

"Twelve," D.C. said, his face turning crimson.

"*Really?* I would've guessed nine. You're almost the same age as my younger sister. Amber-Grace just turned thirteen and thinks she rules the world," the pretty teller said with a smile. "Don't spend all that cash in one place!"

Randi was amazed to discover a pleasant member of the Sutton family, but as D.C. approached, she could hear him grumbling. He wasn't exactly flattered that the woman had called him *little*.

"Hey, have a look at what the cat dragged in," Randi said, discreetly pointing toward the office.

"It's Sutton and that businessman! Told ya this was a good idea," D.C. bragged. It had taken half an hour to convince Randi that they might uncover a few clues at the bank.

"No joke," Randi whispered. "Take a peek at the front door. I think we just hit the jackpot!"

Grouchy old Angus McCarthy had entered the bank. He didn't even glance at the kids as he slowly made his way back to Dean Sutton's office. He was favoring his left leg and using a hickory branch as a cane.

"McCarthy's limping!" D.C. gasped. "He wasn't limping when we saw him by his mailbox yesterday afternoon! He must have hurt his leg sometime after that! Do you think he could be the person I kicked in the cabin? Am I really strong enough to hobble a guy? I'm not even five foot one!"

"So what? Bruce Lee was the greatest Kung Fu star of all time, and he was only five foot seven," Randi noted.

"Then maybe Angus *is* the man that I kicked!"

"If so, we know who's been haunting Rock Hollow," Randi said. "What we don't know is *why*." She watched the three men in Dean Sutton's office greet one another. "I sure wish I knew what they were saying."

"I think this is where I take over," D.C. said. "Come with me."

They inched toward the glass doors and stopped by the

copy machine—a safe enough distance to watch without being spotted.

"Sutton just told them he's been *authorized to double the offer,*" D.C. said. "He said *both you gentlemen stand to make a killing.*"

"Whoa! How did you just do that?" Randi asked in astonishment.

"I read lips. I was born a couple of months too early. That's why I have problems with my lungs and my ears. The hearing aids weren't as good when I was little, so I had to teach myself how to read lips."

"That's so cool!" Randi marveled.

"You really think so?" D.C. asked.

"Yeah. It's like you have a superpower or something," Randi said. She craned her neck to get a better view of the office. "I wonder what kind of deal they're making."

One of the older tellers passed by with a stack of folders in her arms. When she saw the kids, she stopped and gave them a puzzled look. "Can I help you?"

"Uh . . . uh," D.C. stammered while Randi searched her brain for an excuse.

The matronly teller looked them over. "If you don't have any business here, I'm afraid I'll have to ask you to leave," she said. "And the next time you come, please bring a parent."

Randi shot a desperate look toward Sutton's office. The mission was falling apart right before her very eyes.

"They're with me," said a voice.

Suddenly the teller was all smiles. "Of course!" she said. "Just let me know if I can get you kids anything!"

Randi wheeled around to find the businessman's son standing behind her. He was wearing his Boston Red Sox hat and a different pair of expensive jeans. She hadn't noticed how tall he was when he'd helped her up after her fall. He was about four inches taller than Randi, which meant he had at least eight on D.C.

"How's your leg?" he asked Randi.

"Better," she said with a grin. "Thanks for helping me the other day. I'm Randi. This is D.C."

"No problem," the boy said. "I'm Pudge Taylor."

"Pudge?" Randi asked. The kid was as thin as a reed.

"It's supposed to be funny. You know, like calling a big guy *Slim* or a tall guy *Shorty*. So what are you two doing here? Is this what kids do for fun in Deer Creek? Hang out at the bank?"

"What else is there to do?" Randi said with a nervous laugh. How could she tell Pudge they had been spying on his father? "Why are *you* here?"

"Good question," Pudge grumbled, his expression turning dark. "I just go wherever my dad drags me."

"Is he the man in there talking to Mr. Sutton and Mr. McCarthy?" Randi asked, playing dumb.

"Yeah. That's all they've been doing since we got here. Talk, talk, talk."

"What are they talking about?" D.C. asked, and Randi winced. The question sounded awfully nosy. Pudge didn't seem to mind, though.

"My guess is it has something to do with the big resort that's going up."

"Resort?" Randi asked.

"My dad's mentioned it a few times. Then I spotted this in a wastebin next to the copy machine." Pudge reached into a pocket and pulled out a crumpled brochure. It opened up to a map of a town that looked a lot like Deer Creek. But the businesses surrounding the town square had new names—and the vacation cottages and riverfront properties were completely gone. Rock Hollow was an "outdoor sports complex." And D.C.'s orchard had been replaced by what looked like a hotel resort, complete with a golf course. A label at the bottom of the map read, DEER CREEK RESORT . . . WHERE CATFISH IS KING!

D.C. gasped. "This is terrible! We've got to stop this!"

Pudge scowled and snatched the flyer back. "Are you kidding? This resort is the best thing that could possibly happen. You try to stop it, and you'll have to answer to *me*."

D.C. lunged at the boy just as the matronly teller rounded the corner. Randi pulled her friend back before any damage was done, though she couldn't help but wonder which of the two boys would have won.

"I think it's time for you kids to head home," said the teller. "This is a business, not a boxing ring."

"We were just leaving," Randi assured her, dragging D.C. out of the bank.

"That dirty, rotten, no good . . ." D.C. was still mumbling when they reached the sidewalk.

"I guess we know why Sutton doesn't want the festival to happen," Randi said.

"Yeah, he's gonna foreclose on all those businesses and farms and build a resort right through our orchard! And Angus McCarthy and Pudge's dad are helping him do it!"

"Not on our watch," Randi said. "We have to step up the investigation. Time to initiate Phase Two. Dean Sutton wasn't anywhere near the monument when the capsule disappeared. That means Angus McCarthy must be the one who took it. But the sheriff says she can't get a warrant to search his house. So I think it's time we had a look for ourselves, don't you?"

"Are you in position?" Randi asked, speaking into one of the standard police-issue radios that had come with her new detective kit.

"Affirmative," D.C. responded.

It was eleven a.m., and Randi was hiding in the bushes across the road from Angus McCarthy's house. D.C. was back in Deer Creek, sitting on a bench outside of the bank, watching for McCarthy to emerge.

"Give me a shout when you have a visual of the target," Randi said.

"Copy that. I'll keep my eyes open," D.C. replied.

Randi clipped the radio to her belt and waited for a pickup truck to pass by. Then, as soon as she was certain no one was watching, she casually strolled across to McCarthy's lawn. Sheriff Ogle had once mentioned that most people in Deer Creek rarely locked their doors. She hoped that Angus McCarthy was one of them.

The front door of McCarthy's house could be seen from the road. So Randi made her way around the building and tried the back door instead. It opened soundlessly. *Country bumpkins,* Randi thought. *In Brooklyn, no one left the house without locking the doors.* Once inside, she stopped to sniff the air. Her nose picked up a hint of a foul odor—one that seemed strangely familiar, though she couldn't quite place it. The room she'd entered was quiet and dark. The window shades in the house were drawn, and the drapes were closed. A sense of uneasiness washed over Randi. She suddenly felt like she was being watched. *Don't be silly! No one's here,* she tried to convince herself. She clicked on the flashlight and guided the beam around the room. And then she heard something . . . *breathing.*

"McCarthy just left the bank." D.C.'s voice came over the radio that was clipped to her belt. "He's stopped at the Bait 'n' Tackle. He's jiggling the lock. Now he's walking down Main Street. Doesn't look like he's headed your way, but I'll keep you posted."

When the transmission ended, Randi heard a low growl. She

slowly turned the light in the direction of the sound and found herself face-to-face with McCarthy's ferocious Rottweiler. The dog bared its canines, and Randi gingerly took a step backward. The dog went wild barking, bobbing its head from side to side and dripping drool onto the floor.

"Okay, okay, doggie. Don't bite," she pleaded, scared sense-less. How could she have forgotten about Angus McCarthy's dog?

"He's stopped at the Country Mart. He's buying an apple. He's . . ."

The sound of D.C.'s voice made the dog even angrier. Randi slowly dialed the radio's volume down and looked around the room, searching for a way to escape. The dog followed her gaze, then took a few steps in her direction, still barking fever-ishly the whole time. Randi caught a strong whiff of the nasty odor she'd detected when she first entered the house. As the beast drew closer, she finally recognized the smell—it was *skunk*. The dog reeked of it. But that wasn't what had upset the creature. Randi could tell by the bloody footprints it had left behind on the linoleum floor that one of its hind paws was injured.

"It's okay," Randi whispered. She slowly knelt down and stroked the animal's head. "Let me guess. You were chasing Rosebud and you stepped on something that hurt your paw?"

The dog whimpered as Randi reached for the sore paw and took it into her hands. "Sshh," she said soothingly. A cocklebur was embedded in the soft pad of the dog's foot. The animal yelped in pain when she pulled it out. Then it licked Randi's face in relief.

"See, isn't that better?" she asked, carefully dialing up the volume on her radio.

"Randi! D.C. to Randi!" D.C. was shouting on the other end.

"I'm here."

"Why didn't you answer? I've lost sight of the target! Do you copy?"

"*How?*" Randi demanded. "I was only out of contact for a couple of minutes. What happened?"

"My mom showed up at the Country Mart and made me help her unload a delivery of apples. While I was inside, McCarthy got away!"

Randi rolled her eyes. "Well, then, you gotta go find him, D.C. He's old and limping. It shouldn't be that hard."

"Roger that."

With the dog trotting along behind her, Randi started searching the house in earnest. There was no telling how much time she'd have before McCarthy came home. The kitchen was spacious and nicely decorated. The countertops were granite and the cabinets a beautiful maple. Near the sink was a dog bowl with the name BUNNY stenciled on the side. Now that she'd gotten to see the sweet side of the dog, Bunny seemed like the perfect name. She searched the cabinets and drawers, even the refrigerator, but she didn't see anything that resembled a two-hundred-year-old time capsule.

Randi walked down the hallway and glanced into the neatly decorated bedrooms. In one room, she saw a black-and-white photo of a good-looking young McCarthy and his late wife. Beside it was a picture of an elderly man in a pith helmet. It had to be Toot the Treasure Hunter himself. Randi checked the closets and underneath the beds. Still no time capsule.

At the far end of the hall lay one last chamber. The door was open, and Randi peered inside. McCarthy's private office looked nothing like the other areas of the house. It was a complete disaster zone. Stacked on every available surface were newspaper clippings and volumes of dusty old history books. The desk was covered with sludge-filled coffee mugs and ashtrays filled to the brim with cigar ashes.

"Ew," Randi said, scrunching her nose.

She took out her camera and set to work documenting the scene. She was about to shoot a photo of a tiny closet space at the back of the office when a pair of boots caught her eye. *Hiking boots.* She moved closer to investigate. The boots' tread seemed similar the dusty prints she and D.C. had found inside the cabin at Rock Hollow, but the boots that had left *those* prints had been an average size. McCarthy, on the other hand, appeared to have unusually large feet. Randi grabbed a sheet of copy paper and placed the long edge next to the boots for comparison. She knew that the paper was eleven inches long—and McCarthy's boots were several inches longer. She snapped a quick photo, then turned her attention back to the desk.

She settled down in McCarthy's chair and began rummaging through the pile of books and documents. She paused for a look at a few old clippings from the Deer Creek newspaper. The first article Randi examined focused on the town's early years. Randi skimmed it quickly and found the story of Creek Walker and Running Deer, just as Sheriff Ogle had recounted it. The article was accompanied by portraits of the town's three founders: McCarthy's great-great-great grandfather Jed, Liam Sutton, and Sean Prufrock.

As Randi sifted through the other items on the desk, a small, tattered book fell to the floor. She picked it up and examined it more closely. A diary. She opened it to the first entry, which was dated September 18, 1985.

Paw Paw Jed always said that the treasure was buried in the heart of this town. But it wasn't under the . . .

Someone had spilled coffee on the page, and the rest of the words had bled together. Randi thumbed through the book until she found the next legible entry.

Remember how it all began. It began in this cabin—the first building ever built in Deer Creek.

*I'VE PRACTICALLY TORN THE WHOLE PLACE APART AND
NOTHING. IT'S TIME TO START LOOKING ELSEWHERE.*

Randi felt a chill course down her spine. She had to be reading Toot McCarthy's diary! Suddenly, D.C.'s voice crackled over the radio. The signal was breaking up, so she couldn't make out what he was saying.

"I found him! I found him! The Big . . . ish is . . . the move . . . Randi . . . ," said D.C., followed by some words that sounded like "fishing." Maybe Angus was in his bait and tackle shop? "Do you copy?" D.C.'s voice interrupted again.

"Negative transmission. But I'm almost done here," Randi replied.

She flipped to the end of the diary.

*I FOUND THE PRINTS ON THE WALL LAST NIGHT, BUT IT
WAS TOO LATE TO START DIGGING. I TRIED MY BEST TO
MAP THE WAY. AS SOON AS THE SUN COMES UP, I'LL BE
BACK TO THE SPOT WITH A SHOVEL AND A PICKAX.*

Toot found the treasure! And he must have made a map! Randi thought. The final pages of the diary had been ripped out. If one of them had ever contained a map, it was now gone for good.

"Get out!" D.C. cried into the radio, abandoning radio protocol. "Get out now! He's coming home!"

Randi hurriedly snapped photos of the diary; then she placed the book back where she'd found it on the desk. On her way out of the office, she tripped over a chew toy that Bunny had carried into the room. She bumped into a pile of old documents on the side of McCarthy's desk, and they fluttered to the floor. Randi picked herself up, quickly restacked the papers, and ran down the hall.

"He's at . . . front . . . or!" D.C.'s voice screamed from Randi's radio.

Randi swung around to face the front door just as someone on the other side began to turn the knob. She flew back down the hall in a panic, ducked into one of the bedrooms, and slid behind the door. From where she was hiding, she could hear McCarthy's heavy footsteps coming toward her down the entrance hall. ☠

☠ Go to Appendix G to complete the Ninja Task!

CHAPTER THIRTEEN

STUCK

Randi stood paralyzed behind the bedroom door and listened as McCarthy's keys hit a table with a jingly thud.

"Crooks!" McCarthy muttered to himself. "Think they got me right where they want me. Well, I'll show them!"

Randi heard Bunny pad into the living room.

"There's my girl!" McCarthy sounded as if his mood had suddenly lightened.

He whistled as he walked toward the kitchen. "Is my pretty wittle Bunny ready for her lunch?" he asked, speaking baby talk to the dog.

Randi could hear the hum of an electric can opener and the refrigerator door open and close. Then she detected the unmistakable sounds of Bunny wolfing down her lunch—and McCarthy stomping back down the hall.

Randi's heart pounded wildly in her ears, growing louder with every second. *KATHUMP . . . KATHUMP . . . KATHUMP . . . KATHUMP . . . How am I going to get out of here?* she thought, her brow misting with sweat. Fear stabbed at her insides.

KA-THUMP . . . *KA-THUMP, KA-THUMP.* Her heartbeat kept time with the approaching footsteps. *KA-THUMP, KA-THUMP, KA-THUMP!*

At the very last moment, right before McCarthy entered the room where she was hiding, Randi crawled under the bed, barely squeezing herself between dusty old hatboxes and suitcases. It felt like her heart was about to thump right out of her chest when the bedroom door swung open. Bunny bounded into the room, sniffing the floor where Randi had been standing. McCarthy sat on the bed and took off his shoes.

"Oh, sweet Virginia," he moaned. "I do wish you were still here. These sure are troubled times. I never knew there could be such mendacity in this world." At first Randi wondered if someone else had come into the room. Then she realized he was talking to the photo of his dead wife on the nightstand.

Bunny hopped up on the bed to offer some comfort, but McCarthy pushed her back off again.

"Whew, Bunny, you smell plum awful! Why do I have to keep tellin' you not to tangle with that skunk? Rosebud gets the better of you every time." And then the unthinkable happened. McCarthy stretched, yawned, and lay across the bed for a nap. "Terrible day. And it's gonna be another long night.

My old body can't take much more of this punishment," he grumbled, and then he was still.

Bunny trotted over to the door and lay down against it. With her face buried in her paws, she too fell asleep.

You've gotta be kidding me, Randi thought. *That dog's never going to let me leave without waking up the old man.*

She waited until McCarthy's breathing became rhythmic; then she started to crawl out from beneath the bed.

"STOP RIGHT THERE, TRESSPASSERS!" McCarthy yelled.

Randi froze. The mattress springs creaked as he shifted his weight in the bed above. Somehow she'd been caught. Then . . .

"ZZZZZZZZZZ . . . ZZZZZZZZZZ," McCarthy snored. "THIEVES!" he yelled in his sleep, then went right back to snoring.

Randi sighed with relief and tried again to crawl out of her hiding place. Unfortunately, this time she couldn't move. The mattress had sagged under McCarthy's weight and pinned her to the floor. She was stuck. The only thing she could do was wait as the minutes slowly ticked by on her watch. Hoping for a little more breathing space, Randi pushed an old box to the side. The bottom of the mattress swept a layer of dust off the top of the box—and right into Randi's face.

She pinched her nostrils, hoping that the particles would soon settle, but the damage was done. The dust had already tickled her nose. Tears welled up in Randi's eyes as the explosion came closer and closer to the surface. She held her breath to stifle a cough in the back of her throat. But the sneeze was coming, and it was coming fast!

"AAH . . ." She choked it back.

"AAH . . ." The sneeze was pushing its way through. What could she do?

"AACHOO!" Randi finally exploded. Her blood turned cold with fear. She'd literally blown her cover. She expected McCarthy to drag her from her hiding place. Soon it would all be over. She put her head to the floor and swallowed hard, trying not to throw up.

She had failed. She was no Glenn Street. Not even close. Now she would probably be sent to jail. Glenn Street had sent lots of people to prison for breaking and entering. And every time she locked another bad guy away, she'd whisper her catchphrase: *Game Over, Loser!*

Now Randi was the loser.

"Bless you, Bunny," McCarthy mumbled just as the doorbell rang. "Dagnab it!" he growled, pulling himself up to answer the door. Finally free, Randi slid out from beneath the bed and stealthily made her way across the room toward the hall.

The doorbell rang again, and Randi froze.

"I'm coming. I'm coming," McCarthy grumbled, and

opened the door. Randi peeked out of the bedroom and saw
D.C. waiting nervously on the front porch.

"Uh . . . hi, Mr. McCarthy."

"What do you want, boy?" McCarthy demanded.

While McCarthy's back was turned toward her, Randi
stepped out into the hall and caught D.C.'s attention. He stood
frozen, his mouth agape. If he'd had an excuse for ringing the
bell, he seemed to have already forgotten it. So Randi did her
best to help him out. First she pretended to pant like a dog,
then she walked like a person with a leash in one hand.

"I said, what do you want!" McCarthy stormed.

"To go for a walk?" D.C. said, confused by Randi's performance.

"Boy, I'll ask you one more time. What is it you want?"
McCarthy growled.

"I was, uh, wondering if you needed, uh . . ."

Randi threw up her hands in disgust. D.C. wasn't very good
at playing charades. While McCarthy's eyes drilled holes into
the boy, Randi heard another set of footsteps coming up the
front stairs. D.C. was still stammering when Pudge appeared
beside him. "Wha . . . ," he started to ask, but Pudge put a
hand on his shoulder. The boy locked eyes with Randi, who
repeated her pantomime performance. Pudge understood.
While he talked, Randi began inching backward toward the
house's rear door.

"We're starting our own dog-walking business, sir," Pudge

told Angus McCarthy, "and we were wondering if you might need a . . ."

"Your daddy know you're friends with this here juvenile delinquent?" Angus asked the boy.

"He invited me to be part of his business. I think my dad will be proud when he hears."

"Dog walking?" McCarthy harrumphed. "Likely story. Tell your friend to stay off my property and away from my dog—or he'll be sorry he was ever born!" McCarthy slammed the front door just as Randi slipped out the back.

"Whew! That was close," Randi told the two boys as they all made their way toward the road. "Thanks, Pudge."

"Yeah, thanks," D.C. added. "And sorry about this morning at the bank."

"Forget about it," Pudge said. "What were you guys doing to McCarthy's house?"

Randi and D.C. shared a glance. "That's confidential," D.C. said.

"How'd you know I needed help, anyway?" Randi asked.

"I was riding by and heard McCarthy shouting." Pudge paused to pick up the bike he'd left on the side of the road.

"Riding?" Randi asked suspiciously. "Where were you going?"

"That's confidential," Pudge replied with a grin. Then he hopped on the bike and rode off in the direction of town.

"Strange kid," D.C. said as they watched Pudge ride away.

"Yep," Randi agreed.

"Maybe he's not as bad as I thought," D.C. added.

Randi nodded. "I say we investigate as soon as we've solved the capsule case. By the way, I owe you a thank-you, too. I was trapped under the bed before you rang the bell."

"Sorry I didn't get the dog-walking clue," D.C. said. "D'you find anything while you were inside the house?"

"Plenty. First of all, McCarthy's not the worst man in the world. He misses his wife and he's really sweet to his dog. Also, he might be the guy you kicked in the cabin, but I'm starting to think that he might not have been the "ghost" I saw looking at me through the window. I found a pair of his boots in the closet, and they're a lot bigger than the boot prints we picked up at the cabin."

"What about the time capsule?" D.C. asked.

"Nope. Didn't see any sign of the capsule. I did come across an old diary that belonged to Toot McCarthy. I think he might have found the treasure right before he disappeared."

"Did the diary say where it is?"

"No. Looked like Toot might have drawn a treasure map, but it had been ripped out of the book. Probably a long time ago."

"So no capsule and no treasure," D.C. moaned. "We're right back where we started!"

Just then Sheriff Ogle rode past them and stopped in front

of McCarthy's house. Mayor Landers was sitting in the passenger seat of the cruiser. He stayed put while Sheriff Ogle got out and walked up the steps of McCarthy's front porch.

"Do you think she finally got the search warrant?" Randi asked.

They snuck back just in time to hear McCarthy open the door and shout angrily, "I said I wasn't . . ."

"Excuse me?" Sheriff Ogle said, taken aback.

"Oh, it's you. I thought it was those kids again. What do you want, Mildred?"

The sheriff stared down at her feet. "I'm sure you've heard the rumors going round town, Angus. Folks seem to think you had something to do with the capsule disappearing. Now, I'm gonna be honest with you. I don't have enough evidence to request a search warrant. So I'm just going to ask you to let me come in and have a look around your house. If you don't have the capsule, I give you my word that your name will be cleared of all suspicion."

I'm just going to ask? Randi shook her head. *I'll give you my word? Could Deer Creek's sheriff get any more pathetic?*

"Don't matter if you find the capsule or not, Mildred. We both know folks'll still say what they want. They laughed at my daddy; now they're pointing their fingers at me. But I'm going to have the last laugh, Mildred. Just you wait and see!" Then he slammed the door in her face.

"Did you hear that?" D.C. groaned. "It's over."

"No, it's not!" Randi insisted. "Go home and ask your mom if you can sleep at my house tonight, and I'll ask my dad if I can stay the night at your place."

"What are you cookin' up?" D.C. asked, kicking the gravel on the side of the road.

"Phase Three of our plan," said Randi, hoping she'd have enough time to come up with one.

CHAPTER FOURTEEN

LIAR, LIAR

Mei-Ling was in the living room hanging paintings when Randi arrived home. A still life of poppies already decorated the foyer. Now Mei-Ling was holding a painting that Randi's mother had done the last summer the whole family had been together in Deer Creek. It showed the monument in the center of town, surrounded by the brightly colored pansies that Randi's mom had planted herself. Randi was about to rush up to her bedroom when Mei-Ling called out to her.

"Give me a hand, please, Miranda," she said. "Pass me the hammer."

When the painting had been hung, Randi took a step back to admire the artwork. Her mother hadn't allowed any of her art to be displayed around the house, and Randi never understood why. The paintings might have been the work of an amateur artist, but that didn't make them any less lovely.

"What do you think, eh? *Hen hao?*"

Having thumbed through the Mandarin dictionary that

Mei-Ling had given her, Randi knew that *hao* meant good. "*Hen hao*, Mei-Ling. Very good," Randi replied.

"I found them in the cellar and thought it was a shame that no one was enjoying such beautiful art. It was just collecting dust."

"Thanks for saving it," Randi said. She hoped Mei-Ling didn't hear the quiver in her voice.

"You're welcome," Mei-Ling told her. And before Randi knew it, they were sharing a hug. She even let it last for a few seconds before she pulled away. "I know how important it is," Mei-Ling added, "to keep little reminders of the people we've lost. My husband was a carpenter, and I would never get rid of the things that he built. They make me feel as if he's still there."

"My dad threw my mom's paintings into the cellar."

"He doesn't need the paintings to remind him, *mae mae*. This whole town is your mother to him. Why do you think he brought you here?"

"I never thought of it that way," Randi said as she stared at the painting in front of her.

Mei-Ling smiled and scoped out a place to hang another artwork. "I hope you're hungry, Miranda. I'm making my special fish *yi mein* tonight."

"Yi *what*?" Randi mumbled, distracted by her mother's painting of the monument. She took a step closer, until she could read the message engraved on the monument's plaque. REMEMBER HOW IT ALL BEGAN. It was the same thing Toot had written in the diary she'd found at Angus McCarthy's house. What else had the diary said? Something about the treasure being in the heart of the town, but not under the . . . *monument*. That had to have been the word that was missing! Was the message on the monument's plaque a clue to the treasure's real location? Is that how Toot had managed to find it?

"*Yi mein*. It's delicious." Mei-Ling was still talking. "Chewy golden noodles with my secret ingredient: catfish."

Randi could barely hide her excitement. "Sounds great. Too bad I'll have to miss it, Mei-Ling. I'm gonna ask Dad if I can camp out with D.C. tonight."

"Oh, no, no. Not tonight. It's going to storm."

Randi's eyes narrowed. The last thing she needed was a nanny poking her nose in where it didn't belong. "The television forecast said it would be clear and sunny all week."

"You can never trust the forecast. Only trust your body. Before the first big summer rain, my left ankle swells. See?" Mei-Ling said. She kicked out her left foot for Randi to see her bloated ankle. "Well, go ahead and ask. He's in his office. If he says yes, I will save some *yi mein* especially for you."

"Thanks," Randi said. *Now mind your own business.*

Randi bypassed her dad's office and hurried up to her room. Once the door was closed, she dumped the contents of her backpack out on the bed. She grabbed her camera and began to scroll through the evidence photos. The first pictures she examined were the ones she'd taken of Toot's old diary. He seemed to think that the monument's message was a clue to the treasure's location. He'd started his search inside his own cabin—the first house built by the town's three founders, but that didn't seem to be where he'd found it. If only Randi had gotten a look at the treasure map!

Randi went through the rest of the evidence. She found the photo she'd taken of Angus McCarthy's boots. And just as she'd suspected, they didn't match the boot prints that she and D.C. had discovered inside the cabin at Rock Hollow. Who had she seen looking at her through the window? Had someone else figured out that the monument's message was a clue? Had that person gone to the cabin to search for Toot's treasure?

Randi felt like she'd been presented with a giant jigsaw puzzle. The pieces all fit together somehow. She just didn't have enough time to figure out *how*. She and D.C. had only a few hours left to save his mom's orchard. That meant they had to go back to Angus McCarthy's house. This time they'd wait until he fell asleep and have one last look for the time capsule.

Randi tiptoed down the hall to her father's office and listened to him typing while she stood at the door collecting her thoughts. She had to find a way to get out of the house, but she didn't enjoy deceiving him. She'd never kept secrets when her mom was alive. Lately, though, it seemed like the Rhodes family had forgotten how to tell the truth. Her father hadn't even told his own daughter that he was writing again. And Randi had lied about, well . . . just about everything for over a year.

It would have been easier if she'd been born a boy, Randi thought again. Her dad wouldn't worry so much—or try so hard to protect her. If she were a boy, she could have told him about her detective work. They could have swapped crime stories and forensics tips. And she wouldn't have to lie all the time. Randi sighed and brushed that aside. *The capsule*, she thought. *I have to focus on the capsule.* Glenn Street would never let anything stand in the way of a big case. Besides, Randi wasn't really planning to *lie*—she was just delaying the truth a little. She'd explain everything as soon she'd recovered the time capsule. And when she did, she knew it would make her dad proud.

She nudged the door a bit and watched her father working at his computer. *Click, click, click.* His fingers glided across the keyboard, never missing a stroke. Randi glanced around the small room. She hadn't been in the office since the first day of their move. Back then, it had been covered in two years' worth of dust. Now the wood furniture gleamed and sunlight streamed through crystal-clear windows. Oak bookshelves held neatly organized volumes of detective manuals and hardbound copies of the Glenn Street novels. Randi smiled to herself and ran her fingers along the books' gilded spines.

Herb Rhodes muttered something to himself as he tapped at the computer's keyboard with musician-like precision.

Randi plopped down on the edge of the desk.

"What can I do for you?" Herb asked without looking up.

"Oh, nothing. What's up with you?"

"Just jotting down a few notes."

"For a book? You haven't done that in a while. How's it going?" Randi asked.

Herb ran his fingers through his salt-and-pepper hair. "Fine, thanks," he said. He stopped typing and glanced up at Randi. "What do you need, honey?"

Randi's gaze landed on the family photo on Herb's desk. "A lot of people are going to be hurt if the town council votes to postpone the festival, huh, Dad?"

"I hope not. Maybe the time capsule will be located before the deadline. Let's be optimistic. Is that what you came here to talk about?"

"No. I wanted to ask if I can camp out at D.C.'s place tonight. His mom said it was okay with her if it's okay with you."

"Hmm." Herb grimaced. "I've never met this kid, and you barely know him, kiddo."

"He's *great*, Dad," she said in her bubbly little girl voice. "*Really*. He's my *only* friend. We just want to finish working on our secret hideout."

But this time, Randi's father wasn't buying the act. "Maybe by the end of summer, after I've gotten to know him and his family."

"The end of the summer?" Randi grumbled. "I'll be dead of boredom by then."

"I hope not. Who'll help Mei-Ling with the laundry?" Herb said with a smile.

"Then I guess I better call D.C. and let him know I'm not coming," Randi sniped, heading for the door. "Thanks for being so understanding, Dad."

Well, I tried, Randi thought as she walked up to her bedroom. She restocked her backpack, making sure she had her digital camera, spiral notepad, binoculars, evidence bags, and fresh batteries for the flashlight. Then she ran downstairs to the kitchen, where she raided the fridge for juice packs, peanut butter-and-jelly sandwiches, and Mei-Ling's homemade *baozi*.

When she was done, she stopped to stare at a painting of daisies that Mei-Ling had hung on one of the walls. She remembered the day two years earlier when her mother had walked into the kitchen holding that very painting. *Ta-da!* she'd said. *Not too shabby, huh, kiddo?* Randi heard footsteps coming up behind her, and for a moment she was sure they belonged to her mother.

But it was only Mei-Ling carrying a handful of folded dish towels. "I see he said yes," she said, eyeing Randi's backpack.

"Nope," Randi said coldly. "I'm just packing up some gear for tomorrow."

Later that night, Randi was pretending to sleep when her father walked through the house, doing his nightly check. She'd left her door slightly open, and she heard a light tap on the wood.

"You up, kiddo?" he whispered.

Randi peeked out from beneath her sheets and saw him glance around the room. A light breeze blew through the curtains. When Randi didn't answer, he sighed and closed the door.

As soon as the latch clicked, Randi popped out from beneath the covers. She listened for her dad to head back downstairs to his office. Now that he was writing again, she knew that's where he'd be until morning.

Already dressed head to toe in black, Randi pulled on her sneakers and grabbed her backpack. Then she quickly scribbled a note and tucked it underneath her pillow.

> I've gone to look for the capsule and save Deer Creek. If you find this note in the morning, something has gone wrong.
>
> If you find it before morning, mind your own business, Mei-Ling!

With everything in order, Randi snuck out of her room and down the stairs.

When she reached the bottom, she stopped and listened for Mei-Ling. Hearing nothing, she tiptoed across the landing and crept past the hall that led to her dad's office. She'd almost reached the front door, but stopped cold in her tracks when she heard her mother's voice.

"You've reached, Herb, Olivia-Kay, and Miranda Rhodes. We're not home, so you know what to do . . . *beep!*" the answering machine played.

Randi stood frozen while her father replayed the outgoing message over and over again. Her eyes were filled with tears when she finally forced herself through the front door.

D.C. had left his window open, just as Randi had instructed. He was tucked under the covers studying *The Warrior Within* by flashlight.

"Empty your mind," Randi heard him read out loud. "Be formless. Shapeless. Like water. Now you put water into a cup. It becomes the cup. You put water into a bottle. It becomes the bottle. Now water can flow, or it can crash. Be water, my friend . . ."

Randi was about to announce her presence when D.C.'s mom knocked at his door. "You awake?"

"Yeah."

"I know you heard me tell Mr. Sutton that we have no place to go, but I want you to know that we're going to be fine," Mrs. Cruz said, her voice trembling. "I'll figure this out, okay?"

"I know you will," he assured her.

"But for now we have each other, and that's all that really matters." She touched D.C.'s brow, checking his temperature.

"You look a little flushed. Are you feeling okay? Did you have an attack?"

"A small one," D.C. reluctantly admitted.

"You've been running around a lot lately. You need to be careful, D.C. We couldn't keep up with the insurance payments, so we can't really afford a hospital visit right now."

"I'll be okay. I'm just tired," said D.C.

"You know you've got to take it easier than other kids." She tucked his hair behind his ears. "You were in that incubator for a very long time when you were a baby. The doctors said it was a miracle you survived."

"I know, Mom!" D.C. replied, sounding annoyed. "My hearing's been okay since I got the new hearing aid, and this is my first asthma attack in a long time. And I'm twelve, you know. I'm not a sick little baby anymore."

Mrs. Cruz smiled nervously, her eyes misting. "You're right. I'm sorry. Why don't I let you get some rest."

Randi stood outside listening. *We really have to solve this case tonight*, she thought. *I had no idea it was this bad. D.C. and his mom can't even afford to get sick.*

As soon as D.C.'s mother was gone, he hopped out of bed, dressed in the *dobok* that Randi had given him. She waved to him from outside, and he gave her a thumbs-up as he pulled on his backpack and scrambled out the window. When he was safely on the ground, they both donned black skullcaps and snuck off into the night, as invisible as ninjas. Randi hopped on her Schwinn and D.C. mounted the BPX5, and together they rode all the way to Angus McCarthy's house and set up camp behind the old man's pickup truck.

They could see McCarthy inside, moving from room to room. When he settled into a La-Z-Boy chair in front of the TV, Randi trained her binoculars on him. Cicadas and crickets sang in the night. A couple of hours passed and nothing happened. McCarthy seemed to be a bona fide night owl.

"What time is it?" D.C. asked.

"Five minutes later than the last time you asked me."

"Which is?"

"Eleven forty-five," said Randi.

"So, we have fifteen minutes to find the time capsule. Great!" D.C. leaned against the truck. "Can we just go home already? I'm starving to death."

"There are peanut-butter-and-jelly sandwiches in my pack."

"I ate them already. And those sweet little dumpling things," griped D.C.

"They're called *baozi*." Randi turned and gave him the evil eye.

"What? I was too nervous to eat dinner at home. We've been out here for hours. And what if you're wrong? What if McCarthy doesn't have the time capsule? What then?"

Randi chewed on her bottom lip. She had been thinking the same thing. She turned her attention back to McCarthy just in time to see the old man get up from the table.

"I think he may be heading to bed," Randi said, passing the binoculars.

"You've said that four times now. And . . . yep, he just picked up the phone."

"What's he saying?"

"Dunno," said D.C. "His back is turned to me. Wait, he just hung up. He's walking to the door."

McCarthy opened the door and Bunny dashed into the yard. The two kids ducked back behind the truck.

"No, Bunny. It's not playtime," they heard McCarthy say. Randi took a peek and saw that the dog had dropped a chew toy at McCarthy's feet. "Okay. Maybe I'll throw it once for you."

He tossed the toy within a few feet of the spot where Randi and D.C. were hiding. Instead of fetching it, Bunny trotted over to greet her new friend, Randi.

"Bring it back, Bunny," McCarthy called, but Bunny didn't budge. She just kept sniffing at Randi and D.C.

"Go away, doggie," D.C. whispered.

"Sssh," Randi hissed.

McCarthy limped over to Bunny. "What've you found there, girl? D'you corner a squirrel? Find rabbit? Well, go get it, girl!" McCarthy chuckled like a proud father.

As he drew closer, Randi and D.C. crouched as low as they could to avoid being seen. Luckily, McCarthy stopped short.

"Come on, girl," he said, and Bunny bounded back toward

him. "You've had your fun, now it's time for you to go in. Daddy's got a lot of work to do." McCarthy led Bunny inside the house.

"That was close," D.C. wheezed, just as McCarthy returned and made his way across the yard to an old tobacco barn that sat at the edge of the property. As he walked the short distance, he kept checking over his shoulder to see if he was being followed. When he finally reached the barn, he gave one last look and went in.

"He's definitely up to something. Did you see how he kept looking over his shoulder?" said Randi.

"That barn must be where he's hiding the capsule!" D.C. whispered excitedly. "I can't believe we didn't check it out the first time we were here!"

The two crept to the barn's entrance. Randi put her ear to the door to warn them of any sudden movement from inside. "What's he doing?" D.C. whispered impatiently.

"I can't hear anything."

D.C. moved closer to Randi and put his ear to the door. "I can't hear anything either," he said almost sarcastically.

Randi pulled the latch to open the door a crack. The old hinges creaked loudly as Randi peeked inside. All she could see in the dim moonlight was a dirt floor and piles of junk. She opened the door wider, and both she and D.C. poked their heads in. There was no sign of McCarthy. They tiptoed inside.

"He's not here!" Randi couldn't believe it.

"But he has to be!" D.C. argued. "We never took our eyes off the door."

The barn floor was littered with chicken coops, carrying crates, withered fishnets, and old canning jars. There was nothing large enough to hide a fully grown man. McCarthy had just disappeared!

CHAPTER FIFTEEN

THE SHADOW

Randi and D.C. wove around the junk piled on the floor of McCarthy's barn.

"I still don't understand how he got past us," D.C. said.

"I'm stumped, too," Randi admitted. "And there's no sign of the time capsule in here, either."

"Should we go check out his house?" D.C. asked.

"I suppose so," Randi muttered, trying to figure out how Angus McCarthy had pulled off his vanishing act. It was the second time in less than a week that Randi had witnessed someone disappear. The first had been at the Rock Hollow cabin the day D.C. had kicked the "ghost." She'd watched to see who came out, but according to Sheriff Ogle, the cabin had been empty.

Randi and D.C. were halfway across McCarthy's yard when she stopped dead in her tracks. "That's how he does it!" she exclaimed.

"Does what?" D.C. said.

Randi was glowing with excitement. "That's how he disappears! There must be an underground passage between Angus's barn and Toot's cabin in Rock Hollow! They're not all that far from each other—the Hollow's just over the hill from here."

"Which means . . ." D.C. was starting to put the pieces together, but Randi couldn't wait.

"It means McCarthy just went to the cabin. Maybe that's where he hid the capsule!"

With the full moon now covered by clouds, the night turned murky. Randi and D.C. rode fast and hard down the dark road toward Rock Hollow without a word passing between them. A flash of lightning and a rumbling clap of thunder sent an already-shaky D.C. into a thicket of brambles. He hopped back on the bike and caught up to Randi. *Hoo, hoo, hoo, hoo,* screeched an owl, as if warning them both of the night's dangers.

"What should we do when we find McCarthy?" D.C. asked.

"Make him give us the capsule," Randi said. The wind picked up, and the trees showered them with leaves. "Looks like Mei-Ling was right. It's going to storm."

Randi stopped a few yards short of the cabin.

"Maybe we should hide our bikes under some brush," she said. "We don't want McCarthy to look out a window and see them."

D.C. glanced nervously at the woods. The cabin spooked him, but the surrounding forest seemed to scare him silly.

Suddenly he took a step backward and gasped. "There's something out there!" he whispered.

"Out where?"

"In the woods! I swear I just saw a shadow peek out from behind a bush!"

"You're imagining things," Randi said, and her words seemed to summon a spirit. A tall, thin figure appeared between two trees.

"Hey!" the shadow shouted just as lightning illuminated the night sky. D.C. yelped and nearly jumped out of his sneakers. A thunderous boom drowned out his cry.

Randi assumed a combat stance. "Give us the capsule, McCarthy!" she ordered.

"Who?" the shadow asked. As it moved toward them, its features began to take shape.

"Pudge?" Randi asked. "What are *you* doing out here? It's after midnight, and there's about to be a thunderstorm."

"My dad owns this land. What are *you* doing here—other than trespassing on my property?"

Randi and D.C. exchanged a glance. Pudge *had* saved her when she was trapped in Angus McCarthy's house, so Randi reluctantly decided to trust him. "We're looking for the missing time capsule."

The kid checked an imaginary watch. "Little late for that, isn't it? Wasn't the deadline midnight? Why do you think it's out here, anyway?"

"Because Angus McCarthy stole it," D.C. said. "And he's got a secret underground passage that goes from his house to the cabin. We saw him disappear into it, so that must mean he's here—and the capsule might be with him."

"A man came out of the cabin about five minutes ago and headed off into the woods," Pudge said. "It was too dark to see his face. I guess it could have been old man McCarthy. I thought about following him until I caught a glimpse of his shotgun."

"Angus McCarthy just went into the woods with a shotgun?" D.C. repeated. "That's really weird."

"Believe it or not, it seems pretty normal compared to the other stuff I've seen tonight," Pudge informed them.

"What have you seen?"

Pudge hesitated, but he couldn't seem to resist sharing his story. "My dad and I have been staying at that old River View Hotel. . . ."

"The one owned by the Dunkin family?" Randi asked, recalling her conversation with Kate Dunkin the day she and D.C. had rescued Pumpkin.

"Uh-huh. Right now the only guests besides us are those so-called Secret Service agents who've been hanging out in town."

"So-called?"

Pudge nodded. "My dad used to be a colonel in the army, and it made him a stickler about his appearance. He still wakes up early every day to polish his shoes. The Secret Service is supposed to have a pretty tight dress code, but I saw a couple of the agents walking around with mud-covered hiking boots. That's when I started to think there might be something strange about the guys. So I started watching them, and boy was I right."

"What did you see?" Randi asked, feeling a little jealous. She should have been the one to pick up on the agents' muddy boots.

"The first thing I noticed was that they never seemed to be around in the afternoon or evening. You remember ever seeing them between about two and ten p.m.?"

"No," Randi admitted.

"Yeah, that's because they were sleeping."

"Sleeping?" D.C. asked.

"I'm pretty sure that's what they were doing, 'cause around eleven every night, they'd all cram into those SUVs. About ten minutes later, the cars would come back empty. Then at five or so in the morning, the SUVs would go get the agents and bring them back to the hotel."

"Wow, you must have spent a lot of time on stakeout," Randi said.

"What else is there to do in this town? Fish?"

"Good point," Randi said.

"So where do you think the agents were going every night?" D.C. asked.

"Here," Pudge replied.

"*Here?*" D.C. and Randi asked in unison.

"Yeah. I figured I'd tail them tonight. So I snuck out of my room after my dad went to sleep. I got on my bike and followed the SUVs here and saw them drop off the agents at the end of the drive. I had to wait a few minutes before I could go after them, and by the time I got down to the cabin, they were already gone."

"Gone where?"

"Into the woods, I guess. Same place McCarthy must have been heading."

A fat drop of rain hit Randi on the arm. She looked up at the sky and another landed in the center of her forehead.

"We should . . . ," she'd started to say, when the clouds opened up above them. "Run!"

She and D.C. dumped their bikes in the woods, and the three kids sprinted to the shelter of Toot McCarthy's old cabin.

They were sopping wet by the time they'd made it inside. Randi stood by one of the windows and watched the storm tear through the mountains. A million thoughts were bouncing around in her head.

"I don't understand," she said after a few minutes. "How could the Secret Service guys be impostors? How did they manage to fool everybody?"

"Even the mayor!" D.C. added.

"Is that who brought them to Deer Creek?" Pudge asked. "The mayor?"

"He's the one who convinced the president to visit," D.C. said. "The Secret Service guys were sent down to make sure everything was safe."

"Unless . . . ," Pudge started to say.

"Unless the mayor never really invited the president," Randi filled in.

"I don't get it," D.C. said.

Randi's face broke into a wide grin. "Hand me a flashlight, please."

She squatted down and examined the floorboards where she and D.C. had found the dusty prints by the window. She ran a finger over the wood and dipped it in her mouth. Then she closed her eyes and shook her head.

"I should have known," she said. "Remember the day I saw the 'ghost' standing here? There were little tiny ants all over the footprints. You know why they were there? Because the boots that left the prints were tracking *honey*."

"Mayor Landers got covered in honey the day he got chased by Angus McCarthy's skunk!" D.C. exclaimed.

"Which means the mayor was the person I saw standing in the window. He was the one who scared Pumpkin the cat."

"So Mayor Landers lied about inviting the president to Deer Creek. He brought a bunch of fake Secret Service agents to town. They've been up to something way back in the woods. And the mayor's been chasing a mica-covered cat. You want to tell me how all of that makes any sense?" D.C. asked.

Just then, a beam of light shot through one of the cabin's windows.

"Turn off the flashlight!" Pudge shouted. "There's a car coming down the drive."

Once Randi's flashlight was off, the three kids huddled together in the darkness of the cabin.

"Who do you think it is?" D.C. asked. "Do you think they saw our light?"

The car stopped just outside the cabin. Two men hopped out in the rain and sprinted right up to the cabin's front door.

"Yep," Randi said. "And they're coming after us."

The only place the kids could go was the kitchen. But once they were there, it seemed as though they'd reached a dead end. There was no back door—and no place to hide. Then D.C. tripped over an upturned floorboard.

"What was that?" he whispered as he regained his balance.

Randi bent down for a look. Then, with one quick movement, she seemed to lift up a whole patch of the floor.

"You found the entrance to McCarthy's secret passage!" she whispered.

Pudge and D.C. hurried down a ladder that led into the darkness. Randi was the last one inside, and she closed the trapdoor seconds before they heard footsteps enter the room.

"I could have sworn someone was in here just now!" one of the voices said.

"Must have been the ghost," the kids heard the other agent

respond. "I've seen some strange things through the windows of this cabin, but every time I check it out, there's nobody here."

"There's no such thing as ghosts," the first voice sneered. "If you saw something in here, it was probably that fat cat or those troublemaking kids. Next time, you should drag the little brats out and take them back to the caves. There are places down there where no one would ever find them."

Randi heard D.C. gasp.

"My pleasure," the other agent responded with a laugh. "I wouldn't even charge extra."

"Now let's go finish the project. The boss says if we hang out here much longer, people in town are going to start getting suspicious."

They heard the two men's footsteps head back through the kitchen. Along the way, one of them stepped directly on top of the trapdoor. Randi held her breath, hoping they wouldn't discover the secret passage, and exhaled when the men kept right on walking. The kids below heard a faint click. As soon as the cabin was empty once more, Randi tried to lift up the trapdoor. A lock had caught, and they didn't have the key that would open it. They were trapped.

CHAPTER SIXTEEN

A DEADLY ATTACK

"We'll just have to follow the passage and get out on the other end," Randi said, climbing back down the ladder. "D.C., you got your flashlight?"

There was no answer.

"D.C.?" She dropped down to the bottom and switched on her own light. D.C. was standing against the wall, frantically searching through his pockets. "Did you drop it?" she asked before she realized he wasn't looking for his flashlight. He was trying to find his inhaler.

"He can't breathe," Pudge said, sounding alarmed.

"He's asthmatic! The stress has caused an attack!" Randi rushed into action, patting D.C. down. There was no sign of his inhaler.

"I . . . left . . . it . . . ," D.C. said as he wheezed. His face was already turning blue. Randi grabbed her cell phone out of her backpack, but there was no reception in the passageway.

"Sit down," Pudge ordered the other boy. D.C. slid down

the wall, and Pudge crouched in front of him. "Now listen to me, okay?" he said calmly. "I want you to slow down. Breathe in very, very slowly. Good try. Now exhale just as slowly."

D.C. was still struggling. Randi sat down on the ground next to Pudge. "Make your mind like water," she said. "Be formless and shapeless like water. Now you put water into a cup. It becomes the cup. You put water into a bottle. It becomes the bottle."

D.C. closed his eyes.

"Slowly, that's right. Slowly inhale. Slowly exhale," Pudge chanted. "Don't worry. I know what I'm doing. I have asthma, too."

D.C.'s eyes popped back open. "You?" he said, wheezing again.

"Yeah, me," Pudge said.

"Don't stop concentrating," Randi said. "Remember to keep your mind as still and shapeless as water."

D.C. closed his eyes again. His breathing became slower and more regular, and the color gradually returned to his face. After a few minutes, his head slumped forward.

"D.C.?" Randi asked. She reached out her hand to shake him, but Pudge caught her arm.

"He's just sleeping," he told her. "Let him get some rest. There's nothing more exhausting than an asthma attack."

Randi placed her backpack on the dirt floor and gently helped D.C. lie down with his head on top of it. Then she and

Pudge sat with their backs to the wall, watching over the sleeping boy.

"You were great," Randi whispered.

"You, too," Pudge told her. "Where'd you get all of that stuff about *making your mind water*?"

"Bruce Lee."

"Cool," Pudge said. He picked up a flashlight and shined it around. "If I'd known this place had a secret passage, I wouldn't have been so upset when my dad bought it."

"You said he used to be a colonel in the army? When did he become a real estate developer?"

"What?" Pudge asked as if the question hadn't made any sense. "My dad's not a developer. He's *retired*."

"But what about the brochure you showed us? Isn't he planning to turn Deer Creek into some kind of a resort?"

"My dad doesn't have anything to do with the resort. An anonymous rich guy is building it, and Mr. Sutton is helping him buy up as much of the town as possible. He wants to turn Rock Hollow and the mountains behind it into an outdoor sports complex. So Mr. Sutton keeps trying to convince Angus McCarthy and my dad to sell their land."

"I don't get it," Randi said. "You told us that the resort would be the best thing that could possibly happen to you."

"Yeah, because if my dad decides to sell, it means I won't have to live here! Now that my dad's retired, he wants his kids to grow up in a small town like the one he was raised in. But

I've been bored to death since I got here. I've even been wishing my little sisters had come along on the trip! At least then I'd have someone to argue with. There's nothing to do in this town except spy on a bunch of fake Secret Service agents!"

Randi laughed. "You seem to be pretty good at it. How'd you learn to be a detective?"

"Read a lot of books, I guess. There's one series I really love. My dad buys them for himself, but I always read them first. It's got this lady detective named—"

"Glenn Street?" Randi asked.

"How'd you know?" Pudge asked in astonishment.

"They're my favorite books, too. My dad wrote them."

"Your dad is *Herb Rhodes*?"

"Yep."

Pudge seemed absolutely awestruck. "Well, that explains how *you* got to be such a great detective."

"I'm not," Randi admitted. "I couldn't even find a missing time capsule before the deadline. Now half the people in Deer Creek will lose their businesses, and D.C. and his mom are going to get kicked out of their orchard."

"Who do you think took the capsule? You have any suspects?"

"At first I was pretty sure Angus McCarthy stole it. I saw him talking to Mr. Sutton and your dad, and I figured he had something to do with the Deer Creek resort."

"Nope," Pudge said. "My dad says McCarthy keeps refusing

to sell the little bit of land he has left—even though he's about to go bankrupt. I don't know if he's even *heard* about the resort."

"So that leaves Mr. Sutton. But I didn't see him anywhere near the monument when the capsule was stolen. I guess I could have missed him. . . ."

"You didn't. Mr. Sutton was in a meeting with my dad when the capsule was stolen."

Randi sighed. "Then I don't know who could have done it. Glenn Street always asks, *Who stands to profit?* And I can't think of anyone else who'd profit from making the whole town of Deer Creek go broke."

"I can," Pudge replied. "The mystery guy who wants to buy the whole town. I just wish I knew who it was."

"I don't think there's anyone that rich around here," Randi said.

"The treasure," they heard D.C. mumble. "What if someone found the treasure?"

Randi crawled closer. "You okay?" she asked.

"My mind feels like water. *Muddy* water." D.C. kept his eyes closed but managed a weak grin. "If the treasure was inside the capsule, whoever stole it could use it to buy the whole town."

"I don't think the treasure was ever under the monument," Randi said. "I'm pretty sure Toot discovered it right before he disappeared. When I read his diary, it sounded like he thought the message on the plaque was a clue to the treasure's real location. *Remember how it all began.*"

"What does *that* mean?" Pudge asked.

"I think it means that the treasure is hidden where the town first began."

"The story," D.C. said. "Tell Pudge the story about the Indian sisters."

Randi took a deep breath. "Sheriff Ogle says that when the three founders first came here, they were fighting over the land. Then one day, they rescued two Indian girls from drowning. The girls' father was a chief, and he gave the founders a treasure as thanks. So they stopped fighting over the land and started fighting over the treasure. Then winter hit the mountains. None of them had prepared, so they all had to live in a cave. They would have died if the Indians hadn't helped them. When spring came, they started this town, which they named after the chief's two daughters."

"So the treasure must be hidden down by the river where they saved the two girls," Pudge concluded.

"No." Randi felt a bolt of inspiration shoot through her brain. "That's not where it all began. The town began in the cave where they spent the winter of 1813. Before that, the founders had been fighting. They must have had to work together in order to survive the winter. Before their time in the cave, they were enemies. Afterward, they decided to found Deer Creek."

"That's why the fake Secret Service agents are here in Rock Hollow," D.C. said. "They must be searching the caves for the treasure. The only way to get to them is through the Hollow."

"But who told them where to look? Someone must have known that the treasure was hidden in one of the caves. He stole the time capsule so the festival would have to be canceled—and the town would go bankrupt. Then he planned to use the treasure to buy the whole place and turn it into a big resort."

"There's only one person it could have been," Pudge said.

"The mayor!" all three kids cried at once.

CHAPTER SEVENTEEN

SPELUNKING

As soon as D.C. had recovered, the three ninja detectives followed the underground passage until they found the ladder that led to the trapdoor in Angus McCarthy's barn. Randi and Pudge were already running down the road in the direction of Rock Hollow when they heard D.C. calling for them to stop.

"Wait, guys. Maybe we should go see the sheriff before we head to the caves," he suggested.

"Are you kidding?" Randi scoffed. "And let that old jelly bean take credit for breaking the case?"

"Pudge saw Angus McCarthy head into the woods with a shotgun," D.C. pointed out. "He probably wants the treasure for himself—and who knows who he'll shoot to get it. And those fake Secret Service agents probably have a few weapons too. This could get really dangerous."

But Randi wouldn't listen to reason. "If you're worried, feel free to stay here," she said. "Pudge and I can handle the rest of the case on our own."

"I'm not scared!" D.C. insisted.

"Good! Then let's go!" Randi replied.

When they reached Rock Hollow, the kids set off on the trail that led into the woods. The storm earlier in the evening had left the path slick and muddy. Thorns tore at Randi's clothing, and tree branches swatted her in the face, but she was too excited to feel a thing as she forged uphill.

"There must be a hundred caves in this mountain," D.C. said. "How are we going to know which holds the treasure if we don't have a map?"

"Hey, D.C.'s got a point," Pudge said, just as they arrived at a fork in the trail. "How are we supposed to know which way to go?"

"Easy," Randi said. "We just keep taking the trail that sparkles the most."

When she aimed her flashlight's beam at the right-hand branch of the path, all the kids saw were rocks, plants, and mud. Then she trained her light on the left-hand path, and little specks of mineral glowed in the dirt.

"Mica," Randi noted. "The treasure cave must be full of it. The fake Secret Service men have been tracking it out on their shoes."

"That's what Pumpkin was covered with!" D.C. said.

"He must have snuck into one of their SUVs outside the River View Hotel," Randi said. "And then he followed the men up to the cave. That's why the mayor was trying to catch him. He didn't want anyone to come looking for Pumpkin and stumble across the operation."

Randi, Pudge, and D.C. followed the glittering mica path for half a mile until it ended at the dark entrance of a cave. There was no sign that anyone was inside.

"Do you think they've gone back to the hotel?" Pudge asked.

"Shhh," Randi replied. She could hear a faint hum deep down in the cave. "They're still down there. Let's go."

"Are you sure?" D.C. asked.

Randi glanced back at the trail they had taken up the side of the mountain. A tiny circle of light was dancing in the Hollow below. "Someone's coming," she said. "We can't go back now."

Randi led the way, plunging deeper and deeper into the cave. The ceiling high above their heads was black with bats, and they could hear the rustling of leathery wings. A few of the creatures buzzed past them, and one came close enough to nick Randi's ear. The cave's other residents were equally active. Everything around the kids seemed to be moving. Spiders scampered along the walls, and insects crunched under their shoes.

They followed the hum they'd heard outside the cave, descending deep into the underworld. Finally, Randi spotted a light in the distance, and it grew whiter and brighter as they approached. A portable generator and a dozen utility lamps lit a giant cavern. In the center of the space, a brilliant blue lake teemed with blind white cave fish.

On one side of the lake lay a pile of rubble. On the other side were several neatly stacked piles of rocks, each gleaming with tiny flecks of mica. Randi counted nine men hanging out in the cavern. All of them were covered in sweat and glittering mica dust. They must have been moving the rubble from one side of the lake and stacking it up on the other. But now they appeared to be taking a break.

The three kids slid behind a rock pile.

"Fresh water, food, and I bet this place stays the same temperature all year round," Randi whispered. "If the founders had to spend a winter inside a cave, they couldn't have chosen a better one."

"You think this is the cave the founders lived in?"

"Yep. That's why these guys have been cleaning up the rubble. They must think the treasure is somewhere underneath it." She pulled a pair of binoculars out of her backpack. As soon as she took a peek through the lenses, Randi gasped. "I know why they've stopped! They've found a skeleton! It was underneath the rubble! It's got to be Toot the Treasure Hunter!"

The bones were still clad in a denim shirt and dungarees. A plastic pith helmet and a pickax lay nearby.

"Toot must have gotten trapped by a cave-in! That's why he vanished without a trace!"

"Can you see the founders' treasure?" Pudge asked.

"Nope," Randi replied. "But wait just a second! There's something on the wall!"

There were three different handprints on the wall of the cavern, just a few inches from Toot's skull. They'd been arranged to form a circle. It must have been a symbol the founders had left to mark the site of the treasure.

"Good evening, gentlemen!" a man called out in a confident voice.

"It's Mayor Landers!" D.C. whispered.

Randi dropped the binoculars. The dashing, debonair mayor had just entered the cavern in the company of one of the fake agents. He hurried over to the skeleton and crouched down to rifle through its clothes and belongings. When the mayor stood up, he was holding a yellowing sheet of paper, which he folded and shoved into his pocket.

"Excellent work!" he told his henchmen. "Now that you've found him, our work will soon be over. Will someone please bring me a shovel?"

"He's going to dig up the treasure!" Randi gasped in excitement.

One of the men handed the mayor a shovel, and Mayor Landers began to dig. There was only a small hole in the earth when he stopped and passed the shovel back to his man.

"Bury the bones here," he announced as his face stretched into a wide smile. "Then remove the handprints from the wall and replace all the rubble. I don't want any evidence left behind. It should look like no one has ever set foot in this cavern. As soon as you're finished, you'll be paid in full. It's been a pleasure working with you, gentlemen."

"What's going on?" Pudge whispered. Randi didn't have any time to answer before a loud shout echoed around the cavern. She watched the grin slid right off Mayor Landers's face.

"You ain't gonna hide Toot's bones, college boy! You think I'd let you leave my daddy in this cave?"

Everyone spun around. There at the entrance stood Angus McCarthy with a shotgun in his hand.

"What are *you* doing here?" Mayor Landers demanded.

"Came to take the treasure off your hands, Mayor. I believe it belongs to the good people of Deer Creek. So where is it? Give it to me."

"You're too late, Angus. We dug up the treasure yesterday. And for your information, it's *mine!*" the mayor snarled. "I searched for that treasure for almost twenty years, old man."

"You don't have to tell *me*, Mayor Landers," Angus said. "I've been hiding out in that cabin watching you come and go the whole time. Even built a tunnel from my house. But just 'cause you found the treasure don't make it *yours*. This here's *my* land. That treasure was buried in this cave by *my* great-great-great-grandpappy. And *my* father was the one who figured out where the founders had hidden it."

"But I'm the one who finally dug it up," the mayor argued.

"Sure, using the treasure map you stole outta Toot's diary."

Mayor Landers let out a bitter laugh. "You know as well as I do that the map in the diary wasn't much help. It was just an unfinished draft! He brought the real map with him when he returned to the cave." Landers took out the paper he'd stolen from Toot's bones and waved it in the air. "I knew the treasure was down here somewhere, but it took me ages to figure out that there must have been a cave-in inside this cavern. I was the one who paid these men to remove the rubble."

"Cooked up a pretty good story to explain them being in town, too. Secret Service agents, my boot!" Angus spit on the ground to show his disgust. "Bunch a hired thugs is all they are. I knew they didn't work for the President of the United States when the cowards ran away from a little ol' skunk, leaving that capsule sitting there where anyone could tamper with it."

"So *that's* why he set the skunk loose on the mayor!" Randi whispered. "He was trying to prove that the Secret Service agents were phonies!"

"And then the mayor took the opportunity to accuse Angus of stealing the capsule!" D.C. whispered back. "Mr. McCarthy's been innocent all along!"

While Angus and the mayor faced off, another figure emerged from the darkness. The man crept up behind Angus McCarthy, threw an arm around his neck, and trapped the old man in a headlock. The shotgun went off, and a bullet hit the roof of the cavern. Within seconds, Angus McCarthy had been subdued.

"You should have stayed out of this, Angus," the mayor gloated. "But I'm afraid you'll have to pay for that little skunk incident. Your filthy pet ruined my best summer suit. Take Mr. McCarthy away and deal with him," the mayor ordered his employee. "And make sure he won't be coming back. I don't want that old coot causing any more trouble."

Angus's captor nodded and began to drag the elderly man deeper into the tunnels.

"We've got to save Mr. McCarthy!" D.C. whispered.

"What about the treasure?" Pudge asked.

"Who cares about the treasure? They're going to kill Mr. McCarthy!" Randi exclaimed. "Come on! Follow me!"

She and the boys crept behind the rock piles until they were unable to see the mayor and his men. Up ahead, they could see a flashlight's beam.

"There he is," Randi said. "I've got his upper body. D.C., you get his legs."

"You sure I can do it?" D.C. asked.

"You're a lot stronger than you think you are," Randi assured him. "You might not have taken any classes, but you've been training for years."

"By myself," D.C. said.

"No—with Bruce Lee and Jackie Chan. I bet you've seen every Bruce Lee film ever made, right?"

"Yeah, all of them."

"Well, remember how he'd knock down bigger guys using a

side kick to the knee? Think you can do the same move?"

"In my sleep," D.C. replied with a grin.

"You guys are really up for this?" Pudge asked incredulously.

"Absolutely," D.C. replied with new confidence.

"We can't wait!" Randi added.

They slinked quickly and silently toward the man and his captive. When they were less than a foot behind him, Randi nodded to D.C. Then she tapped the thug on the shoulder.

"Wha'?" he cried out in surprise, and his grip on Mr. McCarthy loosened enough for the old man to slip free. When the thug wheeled around to see who was behind him, he was greeted with a lightning-fast punch.

"Arrrrrrrgh," he moaned, just as his legs were knocked out from beneath him.

Once he was down on the ground, Randi delivered a chop to the side of his head that would make sure he stayed nice and quiet for as long as it took them all to escape.

Pudge rushed over. "I can't believe what I just saw! The two of you . . . I can't believe it! I like to think I've got a pretty mean right hook, but that was *amazing*!"

"I told you we were ninja detectives," Randi replied.

"You okay?" D.C. asked Angus McCarthy. He'd taken a tumble when he'd broken free, and he was on the ground where he'd fallen.

"Just twisted my ankle," the old man replied. "But I'll survive, thanks to you three."

"So was it true what you said back there? Have you really been trying to save Deer Creek?" Randi asked.

McCarthy snorted. "Don't make me out to be some kind of hero. I just did what Toot would have wanted me to do. He always loved this town, even though they all laughed at him. That's why he kept looking for the treasure. I was embarrassed by him back then. Now I wish I'd helped him search."

"You and your dad will both be heroes if we can get that treasure back from Mayor Landers," Randi said.

"Yeah, but first we gotta get out of this cave," Pudge pointed out.

"And we gotta do it before the other guys start to wonder where this one went." D.C. pointed at the man who still lay unconscious on the floor of the cave.

"Then let's get cracking," Randi said, taking one of Angus McCarthy's arms. Pudge grabbed the other, and together they helped the old man hobble back toward the cavern.

The mayor and one of the agents were gone when the kids arrived. Eight men were busy dismantling the utility lamps and the generator.

"You guys ready?" Randi asked.

"Yup," D.C. replied.

"Let's do it," Pudge said.

They helped Angus McCarthy down to the ground. "We'll just be a moment," Randi told him. "Enjoy the show."

Then the three ninja detectives stepped into the light.

"Look!" one of the fake agents shouted. "It's those kids again!"

As the fake agents closed in, Randi leaped forward in a gravity-defying jump kick, connecting with the first foe's abdomen. It was so powerful, it sent him reeling backward and into another bad guy.

D.C. took down an agent with a combination head butt and hand attack, then smacked another with a side kick. He spun on his heels to face two more bad guys as they advanced on Randi. But she was ready. She backflipped over the goons and landed behind them on her feet, like a cat. Her movements were graceful. Fluid. Like water.

By the time the agents realized what had happened, Randi was already spinning and kicking low to the ground, smashing ankles, kicking up dust, and exhibiting textbook form on a tornado kick. Pudge rammed the bad guys from behind, and they were down for the count.

The few remaining agents tried to form a human wall around the kids.

Just as one agent was about to strike, D.C. performed an impressive rising kick, catching the guy smack on the chin. Now that D.C. knew how to keep his knees bent, his kicks were precise and hard.

When the dust finally settled, only three people were standing: Randi, D.C., and Pudge.

CHAPTER EIGHTEEN

THE FUGITIVE

Getting injured Angus McCarthy out of the cave was no easy feat. According to Randi's watch, it was three o'clock in the morning when they reached the entrance of the cave and began making their way down the mountainside.

"Hey, what's that?" Pudge said, pointing at the valley below. A line of lights seemed to be snaking down the road from Deer Creek to Rock Hollow.

"Beats me," Randi said. "Fireflies?"

"No—flashlights," D.C. said. "A *lot* of flashlights."

"You kids tell anyone where you were going?" Angus asked. "Looks to me like there are a bunch of folks out looking for you."

"But there's gotta be a hundred lights down there," Pudge said. "If that's a search party, everyone in town must have joined it."

When they arrived in the Hollow, the first thing they saw was Mrs. Prufrock dressed in a long white nightgown, her face covered by a cold-cream mask. She was trampling through the brush, looking for clues while the other citizens of Deer Creek were busy searching the old cabin and its grounds for signs of the three missing kids. Most were dressed only in pajamas and slippers.

"Found 'em," Mrs. Prufrock called out. "And Angus McCarthy, too!"

"Miranda!" her father shouted the second he caught sight of her.

"Dario!" yelled Mrs. Cruz.

"Pudge!" bellowed Colonel Taylor.

The relieved hugs came first, and then the lectures began.

"What in heaven's name have you been doing out here?" Herb Rhodes barked. "You are in *a lot* of trouble, young lady!"

"Dario!" Randi heard Mrs. Cruz screech. "You're a sick little boy! You can't be running around like this!"

"And I am very disappointed in you, young man," said Colonel Taylor.

"Pardon me," Angus McCarthy spoke up. "I know y'all must be pretty angry at your young folks right now, but I think it's only fair to point out that these three saved my life tonight."

"What?" gasped Mrs. Cruz.

"Is this some kind of joke, Angus?" demanded Colonel Taylor.

"Nope. Nothing funny at all 'bout the things these kids did up there in that cave."

"You were in the caves!" Herb Rhodes glowered. "Do you have any idea how dangerous they are?"

"Dangerous for the eight full-grown thugs that these kids left lying on the ground," Angus said with a chuckle.

"You were attacked?" Colonel Taylor asked his son. "Are you injured?"

"Who would attack three little kids?" Mrs. Cruz gasped.

"And what were you doing in those caves?" Herb Rhodes repeated.

"It's a long story," Angus McCarthy said. "And I'll get to it in just a minute. But I think it might be a good idea if somebody here got in touch with the sheriff. I'm afraid there's a fugitive on the loose in Deer Creek."

"A fugitive?" Mrs. Prufrock asked with wide eyes.

"I phoned Sheriff Ogle before we reached the Hollow," Randi's father said. "She told me she'd be here as soon as she was finished making an arrest."

"Who's she arresting?" Mrs. Prufrock asked, her eyes even wider.

They suddenly heard the sound of a police siren. It grew louder and louder as the cruiser approached the Hollow. Sheriff Ogle drove up. When she hopped out, two figures remained in the back of her car.

"I'm glad y'all are here. Since I'm the only police official in town, looks like I'm gonna need to deputize a few of you," she told the crowd. "There are men up on that mountain who need to be brought down in handcuffs."

"Who's that you got in your car, Sheriff?" Mrs. Prufrock asked.

"The mayor," Sheriff Ogle replied. "Knew he was up to something big. Been staking out his house for the past few nights, and I finally caught the sucker red-handed."

"Red-handed?" someone asked. "What did Cameron do?"

"Well, for starters, he's the one who took the capsule."

"When did you figure out that Mayor Landers was the thief?" Randi marveled.

"Same day the capsule disappeared. I saw those phony Secret Service agents running from a little old skunk, and I knew they couldn't be the president's men. The mayor was the reason they were in Deer Creek, so I figured they had to be working for him. And I had a hunch that one of them had snatched the capsule. Of course, I let everyone think Angus was my prime suspect. . . ."

"Wait a second, Mildred. You've known where the capsule was all this time?"

"Sure have. Cameron Landers's house."

"And you didn't tell us?" Mrs. Prufrock gasped.

"I couldn't, Betty. I'm aware I can be a bit of a gossip at times, but this was OPB. *Official police business*. Had to find out why Cameron was going around stealing time capsules."

"Well, now that you've got the capsule, does that mean that the festival won't have to be postponed?" someone asked.

"No, the festival will be held as scheduled," the sheriff said. "But I'm afraid Mayor Landers lied about inviting the president. Those Secret Service agents are just a bunch of thugs he hired to help him steal the Deer Creek treasure."

"How can you steal something that doesn't exist?" Mrs. Prufrock scoffed.

"Oh, it exists, Betty," Sheriff Ogle assured her. She went back to her squad car, and when she returned to the crowd, she was holding a small metal box. "Found this when I searched the mayor's house just now."

Her fingers fumbled with the box's latch. When the top opened, Randi saw two apple-size stones.

"Rocks?" D.C. mumbled.

"Is that the time capsule?" someone else asked.

"Nope. This isn't the time capsule, and these aren't just rocks. You're looking at the Deer Creek treasure."

They watched as the sheriff lifted one of the stones and held it up to the beam from a flashlight. For a moment it glowed a dark bloodred.

"They're rubies!" Randi exclaimed. "I should have known that the treasure would be rubies! The Smokies are famous for them. People used to come to the mountains to pan for rubies in the creeks and rivers."

"How much do you think a couple of rocks that size would be worth?" someone asked.

"Dunno," the sheriff admitted. "Enough to buy a whole town, I'd imagine. That was Cameron's plan. Steal the capsule and bankrupt the town—then use the treasure to buy it himself."

"If Mayor Landers found the treasure, don't the rubies belong to him now?" Herb Rhodes asked.

"He and his men dug them up, all right. But the cave where they found them is on Angus McCarthy's land. In fact, Toot was the one who figured out where the founders had hidden them." The sheriff pulled a sheet of paper from the pocket of her uniform. "Mayor Landers had this in his pocket when I nabbed him. Looks like Toot drew a map to the treasure, so we have proof that the mayor found them on McCarthy property. Now I suppose the Deer Creek treasure belongs to Toot's son."

The crowd gasped.

"What are you going to do with your fortune, Angus?" Herb Rhodes asked the old man.

"First thing, I'm gonna fix up the old Bait 'n' Tackle shop. Then I figure I'll buy my dog Bunny a few nice bones. And then I'm going to sign the rest of the money over to the town. Make sure nobody loses their homes or businesses."

"I'm sorry. Did you just say I won't lose the parlor—" Mrs. Prufrock started to ask right before she fainted and fell in a happy heap on the ground.

While everyone rushed to Mrs. Prufrock's aid, Randi noticed

a small, silver-haired figure standing at the edge of the crowd. Mei-Ling Cooper had been quietly observing the scene.

"You found the note I left under my pillow."

"Yes."

"You checked on me again, didn't you?" Randi asked the nanny. "You've been coming into my room at night."

"The thunderstorm was so loud," the woman tried to explain. "I just wanted to make sure you weren't scared and . . ."

"You got me into a lot of trouble," Randi noted. "My dad still looks pretty mad. I'll probably be grounded for the next six months."

"I'm so sorry, Miranda, but . . ."

Randi put a hand on the woman's arm to stop her. "Thank you," she said. "I'm glad you've been watching over me. Things came pretty close to going seriously wrong tonight. By the way, how did you get the whole town to join in the search?"

"I just *asked*," Mei-Ling said. "I come from a big city too, Miranda. I missed Hong Kong when I first moved to America with my husband. But now I would never go back. In big cities, you can only depend on yourself. In small towns like Deer Creek, we all watch out for one another." Her eyes fell on Herb Rhodes, who was making his way toward them through the crowd. "I'm going to walk home now. You need to talk to your father, Miranda. He was worried sick when we found out you were missing."

"He's always been overprotective," Randi said.

"If there was one thing you loved more than anything else in the world, wouldn't you try to protect it too?"

The small woman left Randi standing in the driveway.

"I know. I know," she said when her father caught up with her. "I'm grounded."

"You certainly are." Herb bent down and took Randi's face into his hands, taking in every freckle on her face. "Do you realize you could have been killed? Do you know what would happen to me if I lost you, too?" His eyes filled with tears. "Every day you look more and more like . . ."

"Mom?"

Randi's father wrapped her up in a hug. He slowly rocked back and forth, and his body seemed to swell with each breath. It was as if he were taking in the entire world. Could it be? Was *he* crying?

"It's okay, Dad. I miss her too," Randi whispered.

CHAPTER NINETEEN

QUEEN OF THE CATFISH

Randi adjusted her new white *dobok* and made sure her black belt was nice and tight.

"Does it look all right?" she asked D.C.

"It's perfect!" he told her. "How about mine?"

Randi's hands shook as she adjusted the boy's yellow belt.

"What are you so nervous about, Randi?" Pudge asked. "This is just a demonstration. A couple of days ago, you took down a bunch of guys twice your size."

"Yeah," Randi said. "But a couple of days ago, my dad wasn't watching."

They heard a round of polite applause coming from the audience on the other side of the curtain. The last contestant had just finished, and it was almost time for Randi to take the stage

"Look who's here!" snarled a familiar voice. "Which one of these losers do you suppose is the girl?"

The three ninja detectives turned. Amber-Grace Sutton had finished her ballet routine and appeared backstage with Stevie

Rogers. Her blond hair was pinned up in a bun, and she wore a fluttery pink tutu, a pink leotard, and a sparkling rhinestone tiara. She looked like a ballerina from a music box.

"You know this is a beauty pageant, right?" Amber asked Randi. "You're not supposed to be wearing your pajamas, you redheaded freak."

Randi replied with a smile. Suddenly her mind was as smooth and still as water. Her calmness seemed to infuriate Amber-Grace.

"My dad lost his bank because of you," she growled. "Today I'm going to give you the beating you deserve."

"Your father broke the law," D.C. pointed out, his voice calm and confident. "He tried to foreclose on my mom's orchard before he had any right. Just because he didn't know what Mayor Landers had planned doesn't mean he was totally innocent."

Amber-Grace turned to Stevie. "You're going to let that little deaf runt speak to me like that?" she demanded.

"Cool down," Stevie ordered the furious ballerina. "There's no need to get nasty. I'm not here to start any fights today."

"Then what good are you?" screeched Amber-Grace, stomping off.

"Sorry about that," Stevie told D.C. once the girl was gone. "She's always had a terrible temper. Hey, I've been meaning to ask—do you think you guys could teach me some of the tricks you used on those guys up at the cave?"

D.C. glanced over at Randi.

"Sure," she said. "As long as you promise to use your powers for good instead of evil."

"Deal!" Stevie said, just as a voice came over the loudspeaker.

"And our next contestant is Miranda Rhodes! She'll be giving us a Tae Kwon Do demonstration with the help of her friends Dario Cruz and Pudge Taylor!"

The crowd went wild as Randi and D.C. appeared on the stage and bowed toward each other. A glimpse of her father and Mei-Ling sitting in the front row set hundreds of butterflies loose in Randi's belly.

"Make your mind like water," D.C. whispered as he lifted a Ping-Pong paddle high above his head.

Randi jumped two feet into the air and slammed the paddle with a reverse hook kick. The audience gasped when she landed in a perfect fighting stance and instantly pummeled the paddle with a crescent kick. As she and D.C. sparred, showcasing an impressive range of hand attacks, Pudge hauled two concrete blocks onto the stage and placed a thick slab of wood on top.

A hush fell over the crowd as Randi approached it. She lifted her right arm, and brought it down in a knife-hand strike. The wood broke into two perfect halves. Everyone in Deer Creek leaped to their feet, cheering and whistling. Randi bowed to the audience and then bowed to her sparring partner.

"That was awesome!" D.C. yelled as soon as they were backstage. "Let's do it again!"

"Hush!" Pudge ordered. "They're about to make the announcement!"

"And the winner of this year's Deer Creek Miss Catfish pageant, by unanimous decree, is . . . Miss Miranda Rhodes!"

Randi threw her arms around her two best friends, and together they jumped up and down. Then Randi returned to the stage to collect her prize. Deer Creek's interim mayor, Angus McCarthy, placed the catfish crown on top of Randi's unruly red curls and draped a sash over her snow-white *dobok*.

But Randi hardly noticed. Her eyes never left the two people in the audience who were clapping, hooting, and whistling the loudest. She was proud to call both of them family. And there was no doubt in her mind that today, they were just as proud of her. ☠

☠ Go to Appendix H to complete the Ninja Task!

CHAPTER TWENTY

THE TOWN TREASURE

"I've never seen anyone make a catfish crown look so good!" Herb Rhodes was beaming. "And that performance! I knew you had a black belt, but I had no idea you were so talented!"

Randi smiled. "So are you going to worry a little bit less about me from now on?"

"Absolutely not," said Herb Rhodes. "I'm your dad. That's my *job*."

"What about your other job?" Randi asked. "How's the writing going?"

"Pretty darn well," he told her. "I guess I just needed some inspiration."

"Time to spill the beans. Are you penning another Glenn Street book?" Randi asked eagerly.

"Nope," Herb Rhodes replied. "I think it's best if we both leave Glenn Street in Brooklyn where she belongs. I've heard a new neighborhood watchdog has taken up where you left off."

Randi raised an eyebrow. "So you found out I used to be . . ."

"Yes, I finally put two and two together and unmasked the Brooklyn vigilante," Herb Rhodes said. "But if you don't want me to worry about you so much, I think it's best if we leave it at that, okay?"

"Okay," Randi said with a laugh. "So is your new book a detective novel?"

"It is."

"And what's your new heroine like?"

"She's tough, smart," Herb Rhodes said with a wink, "and . . ."

Randi could barely contain her excitement. "And what?"

"That's all you get for now."

"Aw, Dad. You're killing me."

Herb Rhodes smiled and brushed a curl away from his daughter's brow. "The galleys will be in soon. I could use a proofreader."

"But that was Mom's job." Randi threw her arms around her dad. There was absolutely nothing that would ever compare to the honor she'd just been given.

"Don't think this means you're not grounded anymore," Herb said with a grin. "And keep in mind, you learned all those detective skills from *me*. So don't think I don't know that Mei-Ling's been letting you slip out while I'm working."

"Who *me*?" Randi said, playing innocent.

"You two are getting as thick as thieves," Herb said.

"Mei-Ling's pretty cool," Randi had to admit.

"Cooler than Glenn Street?" Herb asked.

"Much," Randi said. "I'd say Mei-Ling's the second coolest woman I've ever known."

Randi couldn't remember Herb Rhodes looking happier than he did at that moment.

"Come on," he said. "I think you and your friends have one last duty to perform before we head out to the Cruzes' orchard."

The honor of opening the time capsule had been given to Angus McCarthy. He, in turn, had given it to the three kids who had saved his life. Everyone in Deer Creek had gathered around the monument to see what the legendary capsule contained. Once Randi, Pudge, and D.C. were in place at the microphone stand, Sheriff Ogle presented them with a small hand-carved box. Pudge held the box. D.C. opened the latch. And Randi removed the lid. Inside was a scroll of yellowing paper tied with a faded red ribbon. Randi unrolled the scroll, cleared her throat, and began to read.

"Two hundred years from now, this capsule will be opened. If any Suttons, Prufrocks, or McCarthys live in Deer Creek when this letter is read, then our families may have finally discovered the treasure we always hoped they would find.

"Each of us came to this land to find his fortune. We quickly discovered that we could never survive on our own. Only together were we able to found this fine town. We have been prosperous because our friendship is more precious to us than any riches on earth. Unfortunately, our sons and daughters are now battling over their inheritance—an inheritance we've agreed that they shall not have.

"United we stand. Divided we shall fall. If the town of Deer Creek has survived two hundred years, then its residents have learned that lesson. REMEMBER HOW IT ALL BEGAN and you will have earned your reward.

"Jed McCarthy

"Sean Prufrock

"Liam Sutton"

After the ceremony, the Taylor, Cruz, and Rhodes families gathered at the Guyton Orchard for a celebratory feast. There were apple pies, fish *yi mein*, catfish dumplings, and a mouth-watering jambalaya cooked up by Pudge's mom. Mrs. Taylor had brought Pudge's three little sisters and the family's golden retriever, Sherlock, down to Tennessee a week earlier than scheduled so they wouldn't miss the Founders' Day Festival. She said she still found it hard to believe that her Boston-born son had somehow learned to love sleepy Deer Creek. In fact, Randi heard her telling Mrs. Cruz that the change in Pudge's attitude was nothing short of miraculous. And Mrs. Cruz confided that D.C. seemed much more confident since the events in Rock Hollow. And while his asthma hadn't disappeared, Pudge's advice was helping him learn how to deal with it. Mei-Ling spotted Randi eavesdropping on the two women and gave her a wink. They both knew that Pudge and D.C. weren't the only ones whose lives had recently changed for the better.

After dinner, when the adults were chatting and Pudge's little sisters were chasing one another around the farm, the three ninja detectives slinked away to their hideout. A brand-new computer sat on the table, along with a range of state-of-the-art detective gadgets. They were all thank-you presents from the people of Deer Creek.

The three kids spent the rest of the evening talking about the night they'd spent in the caves. They argued over who'd clocked which bad guy or who'd spent more time acting as Angus McCarthy's crutch. But there was one thing that neither Randi, Pudge, nor D.C. would ever, ever question. . . .

They wouldn't have been able to do it alone.

EPILOGUE

Everyone said that the Founders' Day celebration had been the best in Deer Creek's history. The excitement was over, but Deer Creek would never be the same. Tourists had started trickling in after the treasure's discovery made the national news, and the Deer Creek Restoration Project was busy giving the town a face-lift. More buildings had been restored, and Angus McCarthy's Bait 'n' Tackle shop had received a fresh coat of white paint. A brand-new school was in the works. The volunteer fire station got a shiny chartreuse fire truck.

As soon as they were no longer grounded, Randi, D.C., and Pudge had spent the summer finishing their hideout. By the time the first leaves began to fall, the toolshed had been transformed into a high-tech ninja detective agency, complete with a security guard—Pudge's golden retriever, Sherlock.

A knock at the door brought them all to attention. They waited patiently to see if the intruder knew the secret knock.

He did. Randi hurried to the door and opened it to find her dad waiting at the threshold. Tucked under his arm were three books.

"Hey, kiddo. Thought you guys might like to see these." He handed each of the kids a bright red book embossed with the title *The Ninja Detectives.*

"Is this your new book, sir?" D.C. asked.

Herb nodded. "Fresh off the presses. These are just galleys, of course. That means the book isn't quite finished yet. It still needs a little work. If you don't mind, I'd like you guys to read them and tell me if I've left anything out."

"Thank you for this wonderful opportunity, sir," Pudge said. He was in awe of Randi's dad.

"I'm starting right now!" D.C. exclaimed, turning to the first page.

"Then I'll get out of here and let you three get to work." Herb Rhodes winked at his daughter on his way out the door.

"Why does the cover say the book was written by *O.K. Rhodes*?" Pudge asked Randi. "I thought your dad's name was Herbert."

"O.K. stands for Olivia-Kay. It's my mom's name," Randi said, beaming.

No one said another word until the sun had set and it was too dark to see the pages of their books. That's when they hurried back to D.C.'s house, eager to keep reading about the three young ninja detectives who solved crimes in a small Tennessee town.

As they sprinted through the orchard, Sherlock began to bark. He'd spotted a trespasser hiding in the shadows. . . . But that's another story!

NINJA TASKS

Now that you've helped to solve the first mystery, log on to theninjadetectives.com and learn how you too can become a card-carrying member! The fun doesn't have to end here. Watch kids your own age demonstrate proper forms in Tae Kwon Do (kicking and blocking). And while you're at it, whip up a tasty ND treat! Complete all the tasks and get your Ninja Belt!

And, if you didn't stop along the way to *Clue Review*, here's your chance. This chapter will take you through the process of evidence collection and much, much more. You can try all of these experiments at home. Find a partner—recruit Mom and Dad, Gram or Gramps, or invite your best friend over. Follow the evidence and enjoy the fun!

APPENDIX A:

CONDUCT A STAKEOUT

Things You'll Need:

- Food and water
- Diapers (optional)
- Patience
- A notebook and pen
- Camera
- Binoculars
- A good excuse

What to Do:

» **FIND** a place where you can watch your target without being seen—or a spot in which you won't seem out of place.

» **GET** as comfortable as you can. Stakeouts can take a very, very long time.

» **LIMIT** your food and water intake. You may miss something important if you have to keep running to the bathroom.

» **STOCK UP** on diapers if you can't resist eating and drinking on duty.

» **TAKE** lots of notes. Be sure to write down the things you observe. You may not know how important they are until later!

» **RECORD** any activity that seems suspicious.

» **INVENT** a good excuse to use if you're caught in the middle of your stakeout!

APPENDIX B:

Get Rid of Skunk Stink

Things You'll Need:

- One quart of 3% hydrogen peroxide
- 1/4 cup of baking soda
- One teaspoon of liquid soap

What to Do:

» **AVOID** being sprayed in the first place! Skunks won't attack unless they feel threatened. So if you find yourself confronted by one, be as quiet as possible and try not to make many sudden movements.

» **WASH** your face and eyes with water if skunk juice has made contact with your head. Not just because it's gross, but because it can also cause temporary blindness.

» **DON'T** go inside, if possible. You want the whole house to smell like skunk?

» **TOUCH** as little as you can. It's going to be hard enough getting the stink off of *you*!

» **MIX** up a solution of the ingredients shown above.

» **SCRUB** yourself with the mixture while it's still bubbling.

» **INVEST** in a good perfume or cologne. Otherwise that smell's gonna be in your nose for *days*.

Mrs. Cruz's Chocolate-Drizzled Caramel Apples
(Because You Deserve a Snack!)

Things You'll Need:

- 6 wooden craft sticks (found in cake decorating or hobby shops); Popsicle sticks work too
- 6 tart apples, washed, dried, and stems removed (Granny Smiths preferable)
- 1 14-ounce package of caramels
- 2 tablespoons water
- 8 ounces semisweet chocolate morsels
- 2 teaspoons butter
- Tray or baking sheet lined with wax paper

What to Do:

» **INSERT** one wooden craft or Popsicle stick into stem end of each apple.

» **MICROWAVE** caramels and water in large, microwave-safe bowl on high (100%) power for 2 minutes; stir. Cook for additional 10- to 20-second intervals, stirring until smooth.

» **DIP** each apple in melted caramel; scrape excess caramel from bottoms. Then place on prepared tray. Refrigerate for 30 to 45 minutes or until set.

» **MICROWAVE** chocolate and butter in a large microwavable bowl on medium for 1 minute. Stir.

» **RETURN** bowl to microwave and cook on medium for another 1 to 2 minutes, or until all chocolate is nearly melted, stirring every minute.

» **REMOVE** bowl and stir until chocolate is completely melted and mixture is smooth.

» **DRIZZLE** apples with chocolate as desired. If you have a squeeze bottle on hand, they make great drizzlers.

» **STORE** apples in refrigerator in airtight container. Apples are best if they are served the same day as they are prepared.

» **(ADULT SUPERVISION REQUIRED.)**

MAKE A
FOOTPRINT CAST

Things You'll Need:

- A freshly made footprint in loose soil
- A shoe box
- 1 small bowl or cup
- Small twigs or Popsicle sticks
- 1-pound box of powdered spackle
- 8 ounces of water
- 1 small paintbrush
- 1 bottle of pump hairspray
- 45 minutes of patience

What to Do:

» **FIND** or make a footprint in loose soil.

» **MIX** water and spackle mix (until it has the consistency of pancake batter).

» **SPRAY** the print with pump hairspray. Let stand for five minutes or until print is hard.

» **CUT** out the bottom of the shoe box, then place box around footprint.

» **PUSH** dirt up around the outside of the shoe box to seal any holes so the plaster mix doesn't leak out. (Place twigs at base if needed for extra hold.)

» **POUR** plaster in at one end of the contained area, letting it run into the shoe impression slowly, until the print is covered in plaster.

» **WAIT** forty-five minutes or until completely dry.

» **UNCOVER** print and lift.

» **USE** the paintbrush to gingerly dust debris from your cast. After it dries for twenty-four hours, rinse lightly with water to remove the remaining dirt.

NASTY STAIN AND PRINT DETECTION

Things You'll Need:

- One black light (inexpensive devices can be purchased at many drugstores or hardware stores)
- Petroleum jelly
- Spit (optional)

What to Do:

» **PERFORM** your experiment in a room that you can make perfectly dark (a bathroom is ideal).

» **DIP** a finger into the petroleum jelly. Leave a few petroleum-jelly-covered fingerprints on a surface of your choosing. With the lights on, the fingerprints should be invisible.

» **SWITCH** off the regular light and turn on your black light. The fingerprints you just left will instantly glow blue.

» **TRY** the same experiment with a bit of saliva. Both urine and spit will be invisible under regular lights. Under a black light, however, they will be a bright, glowing yellow.

Collect a Dusty Footprint

Things You'll Need:

- A roll of packaging tape (must be transparent)
- A piece of black poster board
- Scissors
- A sneaker
- A nice, dusty surface (could be a floor, table, desk, etc.)

What to Do:

» **FIND** a very dusty surface and place your sneaker firmly in the center of it.

» **REMOVE** the sneaker. (You should see a nice impression of the shoe.)

» **CUT** about four strips of tape and connect them. (It should be enough to cover the print.)

» **PLACE** the connected tape over the dusty print.

» **PRESS** and lift. (The print should adhere to the tape.)

» **PLACE** the tape on the black poster board.

» **VOILÀ!** You should have a nice dusty footprint.

Eavesdropping

Things You *May* Need:

- Headphones
- A water glass
- A disguise

What to Do:

» **GET** as close as you can to the conversation you'd like to hear. This is easier if the people don't know you. Just try your best to blend into the background.

» **CONSIDER** wearing a disguise if you're eavesdropping on people who might know or recognize you.

» **PRETEND** to be busy.

» **DON'T** look at the people having the conversation.

» **WEAR** headphones and bob your head to imaginary music. Or pretend to be on the phone.

» **FIND** a water glass if you're attempting to listen through a wall. Place the open end of the glass to the wall and press your ear to the closed end. It's an old trick, but you may be surprised how well it works.

PRUFROCK'S
FIVE-MINUTE ICE CREAM
(WHEN A CASE IS OVER, YOU DESERVE A REWARD)

Things You'll Need:

- 1½ tablespoons sugar
- ½ cup of whole milk (for real ice cream consistency)
- ½ teaspoon vanilla extract (see other flavors below)
- Lots of ice (crushed ice works better)
- 8 tablespoons rock salt
- 1 pint-size plastic zipper bag
- 1 gallon-size plastic zipper bag
- 1 spoon
- An ice cream cone (if you desire)

What to Do:

» **TAKE** the small bag and add sugar, milk, and vanilla. Seal it.

» **TAKE** the large bag and fill it with ice and rock salt.

» **PLACE** the small bag inside the large bag. Seal it.

» **SHAKE,** shake, shake! (Until mixture is ice cream.)

» **OPEN** bags, and spoon out or pour into cone. ENJOY!

» For chocolate-flavored ice cream, add ½ teaspoon of sweetened cocoa powder instead of the vanilla.

» For strawberry-flavored ice cream, add ½ teaspoon of sweetened strawberry powder instead of the vanilla.

» For orange/vanilla dream, add ½ teaspoon of powdered sweetened orange drink mix in addition to the vanilla.

» (For all these additional flavors, use only 1 tablespoon of sugar.)